Upside Down

by

Janet Ollerenshaw

Dedication

This work is dedicated to my cousin,
Adam Mallory Farmer
(1957 – 2016)
Love – Happiness - Joy – Friendship

I am inordinately proud and honoured to have known and loved a
very special person who was truly

"A gift from God"

His light, love, acceptance and purity of heart shone throughout his
life
and spilled into the lives of all those who met him.

Acknowledgments

My heartfelt thanks go to my parents who have supported me in every venture I have undertaken and who have unconditionally loved me, my children whose acceptance of their slightly 'crazy' mother has allowed me to demonstrate my craziness in writing, my teaching colleagues and fellow students who gave me the confidence to write and my brothers who made me stronger than I believed I could be.

In particular, I thank Mark, without whose constant encouragement, love and unfailing enthusiasm, this work and its predecessor may never have materialised.

To all of you and to the many others who have made possible the production of these books and the realisation of a dream, I give you my love and everlasting gratitude.

Pearly white iridescence, perfectly formed, exquisitely perfumed
and nestled at its heart, a solitary diamond dewdrop;
the aged rambling rose put forth
a single bloom.

Chapter One

He was totally absorbed. To anyone else, he was just a grubby child playing in the sticky wet mud. Nevertheless, for him it was a whole other world, a universe in which he was God and it was for him to decide who lived and who died, what went where and how it would all begin and all end. The small shiny dung beetle could not escape the prodding poking stick which constantly thwarted its attempts to scurry to the drier edges of the puddle and bury itself in escape from its tormentor. It wasn't that the small boy wanted to kill. Quite the opposite, he wanted to control; to be the ultimate decision maker, the all-seeing eye, the omnipotent ruler of this tiny universe.

"Timophy!" Carrie's call came as he knew it would, breaking the spell of his focus and marking the end of another day. He scooped the beetle into a matchbox and shoved it deep into his back pocket. Attempting to wipe the mud from his knees, he succeeded only in spreading it further across his skin and clothing as he smeared the dirt from his hands onto his jacket and down the sides of his shorts.

Gazing from her upstairs window, Rosa wondered for the umpteenth time, where this son of hers had come from. Of course she knew that he was hers; she vividly remembered the agony of his birth. It was a test of endurance that she had determined never to repeat. Not that the resulting joy in her new-born son hadn't made the whole traumatic time worthwhile. Demanding and overtly demonstrative at times, he exhausted her with his boundless energy, and yet he was the apple of her eye and she would not have changed him for the world. Nevertheless, there were times when she found him a puzzle; an enigma, when, unlike many young children, he would play happily for hours on end, by himself. Totally absorbed in some mysterious and fascinating activity in which he needed no one and nothing, he was content and isolated in his own little world. Peopled with small creatures and imaginary foes, he fought battles, rescued weakened allies and visited places that she could not even dream of. Try as she might she could not distract him from his play when he was so engaged. Only Carrie could break the spell and insist he come to eat, to sleep, to wash or to prepare to go out with the family.

Short, dumpy, moonfaced and smiling an infectious toothless grin, Carrie spread happiness wherever she touched. Academically challenged and physically weak, Carrie, like many of her kind, met whatever life brought with stoicism and courage born of innocence and blind faith. A young woman with Down's syndrome who retained her inner child, she managed herself remarkably well and caused little concern to Eleanor, her adoptive grandmother, or Shane, her step-brother who loved her with a fierce, protective, love which did not allow for teasing, bullying or any other form of abuse of his sister.

The years had been kind to Eleanor and she looked much younger than her age although her gradually shrinking body was slow to obey her commands and her hands shook a little, making the teacup rattle on its saucer as she took it carefully from Rosa's well-manicured fingers. Afternoon tea was a habit they had formed early in their relationship and it remained a custom which brought them together once a day in the privacy of Eleanor's rooms, allowing them time to discuss the family, current affairs and any other business that needed their combined attention. Today, Rosa wanted to discuss her concerns for Timothy. Soon, he should begin his formal education and Rosa was not at all sure that the school Simon, her husband and Timothy's father, had chosen, was the most appropriate for her son's needs.

Niceties dispensed with - the weather, their health, the neighbours - Rosa took the fine porcelain cup from Eleanor and placed it carefully on a side table. She took Eleanor's hand in her own and absentmindedly stroked the soft yet wrinkled and veined skin. Eleanor placed her other hand over Rosa's and leant forward, "What is it my dear?" she asked. Rosa breathed deeply and smiled into Eleanor's grey eyes, "Timothy," she began, but before she could continue, she was interrupted by a sudden ring of surprisingly strong laughter from her surrogate mother-in-law.

Rosa was second wife to Simon. His first wife, Tam, had died childless after a long illness and a troubled lifetime. Tam was the daughter of Eleanor's sister, Jen, who had died in childbirth. Since the then motherless child was also apparently fatherless and alone in the world, Eleanor had raised her niece as her own and had similarly embraced the two children that Tam and Simon had adopted. Carrie and Shane were as much hers as they had been Tam's and she loved them fiercely and protectively. When Rosa came into their nest, closely followed by little Timothy, the family had simply opened its hearts and arms wider and drawn them in completely as they accepted them into their lives.

"Oh but I should have guessed," she gasped as the laughter subsided and, serious once again, she composed herself to listen to Rosa's concerns.

***

Simon missed Tam. Oh he loved Rosa and was more than content in this second marriage and all the joys that his wife and son provided him, but he missed Tam's serenity and other worldliness. She had been able, with a smile, to calm the most tumultuous of storms and her presence had spread balance and equilibrium wherever she went. Rosa, whilst beautiful and good hearted, and who likewise loved him unconditionally, brought other tensions and a wild streak of independence into their relationship. She had insisted on resuming her career in the fashion industry soon after Timothy was born and Simon's dreams of a full-time mother to his son were soon dashed. Of course Eleanor had stepped into the breach and Elsa had been a godsend to them all. How would they have managed without her? And no, he didn't resent Rosa for her choice; it was what she had to do and he understood the importance of it for her. She was very successful and he was proud of her achievements. Nevertheless, he missed Tam and was often to be found sitting on the park bench that had been a favourite haunt of hers. Here in the quiet and fresh air, he could meditate and allow the memory of her spirit into his soul wherein her oil was balm to his heart, soothing away the stresses of

7

everyday life in a somewhat crazy and definitely unconventional family. It was this unconventionality that, to his mind, argued for traditional and conventional schooling for his son. He had never expected to have a son of his own and he was still amazed that at the ripe old age of fifty six he had become a father. Now sixty two, he adored Timothy although he didn't pretend to understand him. Just as Rosa did, he found his son puzzling and something of an enigma. However, he could recognise and appreciate his innate intelligence and was anxious that it should be channelled and nurtured so that it was not lost as was so often the case with young people whose potential is crushed by society's expectations and short-sighted, misplaced importance.

The school Simon had chosen was a Preparatory school with an associated Kindergarten. Timothy could begin attending in September when he would be just six years old. Although expensive, the school would provide him with the basic essentials in a protected and structured setting where he could associate with like-minded children and develop accordingly. However, Rosa was not comfortable with the idea of this elitist environment and would much prefer that he attend the local primary school and make friends with children from the village. She felt that it would give him a much sounder grounding in the ordinariness of local society and a wider range of abilities and opinions upon which to base the formation of his own views on life and the world around him. He was already somewhat insular and did not mix well with other children, or adults, preferring his own company and that of his imaginary friends. It had become something of a barrier between them and Rosa was anxious to find a way to compromise and come to an agreed and acceptable alternative arrangement. Hence her desire to talk to Eleanor, who was wise and experienced in the ways of the world and whose counsel Rosa valued highly.

***

Rivulets ran down the inside of the window as the steam condensed on the cold pane. Water collected in small puddles on the marbled sill and trickled gently from the edge and onto the floor. Bubbles obscured the small blonde and pink figure as he lay completely submerged under the hot water of the bath, his lips clamped firmly around a plastic straw as he breathed in, through his mouth, the warm moist air of the bathroom. The mud from earlier in the day sloughed from his body and rested on the enamelled bottom of the bathtub where its grittiness rubbed on his skin. He liked the roughness, and the heat of the water, and the bubbles, and the steam. Here he could imagine he was entirely alone in an Illyria of his own making; with no outside interruption or interference. He wished he could fill the bathroom with free flying exotic birds and insects, and the bath with little fishes; but of course they would not survive in the heat. Just as when playing in the muddy puddles outside, he was completely happy and needed nothing and no one to improve his situation.

"Time for out, Timophy." Carrie appeared through the misty fog, in her arms a large, warmed fluffy towel, "Upsy daisy." She held out the towel as he leapt into her arms and she bundled him into its folds. He nuzzled into her small but plump softness, tired from his day's play he was ready to sleep and welcomed the summons to his bed. Unlike many children, his sleeping hours were as much to be enjoyed as his time awake. In his dreams he visited other places and experienced other times both of this world and of another. Of course he could not explain any of this to his elders; indeed he did not even try to understand or expand on any of it, he simply enjoyed all that life brought to him, without question or reservation.

Bounding into his cosy bed, he was immediately joined by the aptly named Snowball; a small, white, very fluffy canine whose one end was almost indistinguishable from the other, witnessed only by a protruding wet pink tongue at one end and the whirling stump of a tail at the other. Within minutes of Carrie beginning to read in a sing-song tone that hinted at recital rather than reading afresh, Timothy was asleep, his roseate cheeks glowing with health and hot water, his blonde curls clinging damply to his neck and ears and his soft breathing making his little chest rise and fall evenly and regular. It was to the top of this young head that Rosa bent to kiss her son, breathing in his fresh perfume of innocence and simplicity and pausing to whisper, "I love you my boy child."

As she rose and turned she saw Simon standing in the doorway looking in on his wife and child. She smiled broadly and indicated that he too should come to the bedside. He did so and the proud if perplexed parents stood together, hand in hand, gazing at the child they had created and loving him. Neither one knew what was in store for their progeny although, had they known, there was nothing either of them could have done to change his destiny.

Chapter Two

Mud oozed squishily up through the gaps between his toes as he plodded stoically across the mud flats and out to the stranded lobster pots. Ignoring the cold and wet wind which bit into his face and hands, he was determined to complete the day's work before dark. Trousers rolled up to above his knees, bare footed and covered with an oilskin cape and sou'-wester, the water dripped steadily from the brim, onto his nose and chin and splashed onto the squelching surface below where it joined the retreating surf which gradually threatened to re-cover the mud and hide the occupied pots for another eight hours or so. Not for the first time Tom wondered why he had come to this Godforsaken place and even more, why he had agreed to help his uncle with this impossibly hard task. And as he asked the question so he answered it. It was simple really. Money! Oh he could try to convince himself with all the usual flippant answers about doing favours, supporting, helping out or familial loyalty but the truth was he needed the money. How else was he going to raise enough to pay the fees? It was all very well for those with rich parents who could pay their way with little or no problem. However, for him it was not so easy. Both parents were absent, he didn't like to say they were dead, but in truth they were. He was alone in the world except for his uncle and aunt and that obnoxious tart of a cousin who constantly plagued him with unreasonable demands to escort her to whichever night club or rave she currently wanted to attend. An unpaid escort or chaperone is all he was. She used him as did everyone else. And he was too weak, too afraid of total abandonment, to say no.

He stumbled on until he reached the first of the line of pots, strung out across the muddy estuary like incongruous fairy lights on an unlit tree. He hauled the pot up and opened the top in order to put in his rubber gloved hand and remove the limp lobster which quickly became an angry aggressive alien as he pushed it roughly into the wet sack on his back. Speed was the essence, both for avoiding damage to himself and for getting the lobster into the restaurants in the best condition for subsequent eating.

An hour later a bedraggled figure could be seen making his way back across the now wetted mud. Six inches deep, the water tugged at his bare legs and slowed his progress which was already hampered by the heavy and overfull sack on his back. The rain, which continued to poor down incessantly, further dampened his spirits. It was only the thought of a hot shower, a hot toddy and an evening without the 'tart' that gave him the motivation to finish this terrible task as quickly as possible.

***

Sandra sighed and glared at the reflection glowering back at her from the ancient spotted mirror hanging precariously from a worn string hooked over a rusty nail protruding from the side of an equally ancient wardrobe. For the millionth time she asked herself why she had been blessed with such wiry, black and curly hair which didn't go with her alabaster complexion. Why she looked so much nicer with it straight! Those little curls that insisted on falling over her forehead irritated her extraordinarily and in a fit of pique she snatched up her nail scissors and snipped them off. Immediately she realised she had made a mistake. Now she just looked plain stupid. And it was at this point that the tears came.

There was a light tap on her door. Surprised, since no one ever bothered with her unless they wanted her to do something, she smudged her tear-stained face by wiping her sleeve across her eyes and, sniffing mightily, she opened the door just a crack.

"Are you ok?" came the gruff enquiry, "I thought I heard someone upset." It was very apparent that she was not 'ok' but she nodded tersely and was about to close the door when he noticed the maimed fringe and stepped forward into the lighted room. "Oh dear!" he exclaimed, "What happened?" The unexpected kindness and his obvious concern threw her off guard and the tears flowed freely

12

whilst her shoulders shook with heart wrenching sobs. Unthinking and instinctively he threw his arms around her slight body and held her to him until the deluge eased, the shaking ceased and his cousin regained some semblance of composure. He was at a loss as to what to say or do but her predicament was clear. He couldn't stick the hair back on but he could help her to disguise her foolish error of judgement. Quick thinking and improvisation was needed. Taking a scarf from the back of her chair he neatly folded it into some semblance of a bandana and wound it around her head, tying it carefully underneath the hair at the nape of her neck. She, for the first time ever, beamed at him; the genuine smile lighted her young face and for a moment her inner beauty shone. For an instant he was taken aback at her youth and innocence but the illusion was quickly shattered as she rapidly repaired her smudged make up, applied too much bright pink lipstick and grabbed her coat and bag as she hurried out of the door. "Ta cuz!" she yelled as she disappeared down the street toward the bus stop.

"You're welcome," he muttered to her retreating back and, sighing to himself, made his way to the bathroom which was half buried under piles of wet towels, strewn with lacy underwear and decorated with random items of clothing thoughtlessly discarded over every square inch of floor and surface. Scooping up together all the extraneous items, he shoved them through the door of his cousin's room before closeting himself in the soon locked bathroom with his now not so hot toddy, the latest copy of FHM and with the intention of remaining there for as long as possible.

***

Several hours later; long after his aunt and uncle had retired for the night, and whilst he was lying flat on his back on the hard and sparsely covered bed, he was trying to convince himself that he was content with his lot and attempting to fall asleep. The first crash had him sitting bolt upright and very wide awake. The second had him racing down the stairs, having grabbed the nearest thing to hand, which happened to be an umbrella, to use as a makeshift weapon.

"Burglars!" had been his first thought and as he reached the bottom step it occurred to him to wonder what exactly he thought he could do with an umbrella!

Beslippered, Uncle Joe soon stumbled down the stairs after him, tying the belt of his tartan dressing gown as he came and whilst Tom checked the kitchen and back door, Joe went through to the living room to make sure there were no intruders in there.

The place was deserted. However, just as they were about to blame the local cats or urban foxes for causing a disturbance, they both heard it. A faint moan emanated from somewhere near the bottom of the big old oak front door where the letter box was situated. Tom had always thought it such a silly place for a letter box. Why the poor postman and paper delivery kids always had to put down their bag and kneel in order to post the mail through their door. And to cap it all, on the inside, his aging aunt and uncle also had to bend to the floor in order to retrieve said mail. One day he would change it for them... maybe. Nevertheless, we digress and on this occasion the low level aperture served a different purpose. Tom quickly knelt down and peering through the small opening, saw the edge of the scarf which he had a short while ago used to disguise his cousin's faux pas. Carefully he opened the door and as he did so the very drunken, semi-conscious body of his young cousin fell from sitting against the door to lying across the doorstep. He scooped her up into his strong arms and with Joe leading the way he carried her upstairs and lay her on her bed. She was dirty with vomit, mud and other unidentifiable substances and she smelled of alcohol and some sickly sweet aroma which Tom did not recognise but instinctively knew was neither good nor wholesome.

Joe soon fetched Aunt Aggie who tutted and huffed in a business-like fashion and shooed the two men away so that she could undress and cleanse her wayward daughter. This daughter had been such a joy to them both; an unanticipated and wonderful gift to the surprised and aging parents. Who would have thought that they should produce such a child in their late forties? But produce her they did and they raised her and loved her with a fierceness borne of unexpected riches. Small wonder then that Sandra became spoiled and demanding. Her parents' indulgence had resulted in a typically aggressive and truculent teenager although underneath this veneer resided a heart of gold and a foundation of respect and honour. Attributes which would stand her in good stead in the years to come when her wildness was dissipated and her abundant youthfulness tamed.

Having cleansed her and clothed her in a clean fresh nightshirt, Aggie bent and tenderly kissed the hairless forehead of her beloved daughter. There would be time for recriminations later.

Chapter Three

"Private Thomson!" the order barked across the parade ground and he came to an abrupt halt, clicking his heels in the way he'd been drilled and drawing his right arm up smartly to attention. "Sir, yes Sir!" he responded automatically. His parade uniform was stiff with starch and polish and he moved with the robotic actions of a plastic toy. His expression inscrutable; he was determined not to let his face crack into the habitual irresistibly infectious smile that usually crinkled the corners of his mouth and eyes.

"Come with me," ordered the officer. Although not unkindly said it certainly did not invite refusal and so Private Thomson, or Tomo as he was more readily known, followed dutifully as he was led into the austere and sparsely furnished room that had once served as the Butler's parlour in this big old house.

"Sit!" and he did; sinking into the surprisingly soft leather armchair which was drawn up close to the meagre fire that kept the chill from the room. Sergeant Stanton removed his jacket and donned a pair of leather slippers before similarly sinking into the second chair situated opposite the first. So this was to be an informal conversation. Tomo relaxed just a little, although he was never unguarded in his father's presence, and undid the restrictive buttons from his neck to his waist. He leaned back in the chair and waited, knowing of old that his father would speak when he was ready to and not before or until.

Very few, if any, of his peers and equals knew of his relationship to Sergeant Stanton. Here was the absent father personified. He was an army man through and through and nothing, not even his own sons could have kept him from his career. In spite of his dreams of grandeur and advancement he had remained in the lesser ranks for in reality he was not made of the stuff of leaders but of those who follow orders. So 'Sergeant' he remained; albeit held by those who knew him, in high regard and respected for his age, experience and

16

dedication to his chosen field. He was not, however, a kind man; he did what had to be done with as little fuss and palaver as possible. If that meant he needed to be short and brusque then he was so in a business-like and officious way and without any unnecessary niceties either in praise or rebuke. Everything was matter of fact in his eyes and he was the least romantic person one could ever meet. This apparently cold-hearted attitude had even extended to his wife and his dog – they were useful commodities and provided occasional entertainment but, for the most part, they were simply a convenience to be endured. Thus it was that he met his first born son with surprise. Here were emotions and feelings that he could not handle and so, after the birth of a second son, he simply opted out, leaving his wife, Ellen, to raise the children single-handedly. Not surprising then that she left him and married a gentleman who knew how to woo, nurture and cherish his wife. The children's names were changed and so it had been relatively easy for Private Samuel Thomson to remain apparently unconnected to Sergeant Stanton.

"Well young man," his gruff voice was much softer than the parade ground bark, "I have to admit I didn't think you'd come through as well as you have. I'm actually rather proud of you although there are still areas where you leave yourself weak and somewhat vulnerable." A long pause ensued, wherein Tomo gazed studiously at the flickering flames of the fire and his father tapped his fingers impatiently on the arm of the chair. Neither of them comfortable in this conversation and both were wondering how to change the subject without having actually addressed the issue at stake.

"How is your…"

"Where will you…" both began at the same moment and unexpectedly their eyes met as each looked up to clear the way for the other to continue. Dark brown eyes drilled into clear deep blue and for a brief and silent second a powerful connection held the two men in an unbreakable bond of fraternity. Not love, but something deeper and more fundamental; a sharing of more than flesh and blood; a meeting of spirit and soul.

A little shaken by the unexpected communion, Tomo broke the bond first with a short bark of laughter which the incongruity of the situation drew from his incorrigible sense of humour. Sgt Harry leant back in his chair and visibly relaxed.

"You know I could get you an office job here somewhere… Where you'd be safe… I don't think you're made of front-line stuff… my boy." His dialogue, punctuated with pauses and hesitations, continued, "You're too much like your mother; soft and sentimental. Now, that brother of yours, well he's quite a different matter. Pity he didn't want to join up too. Still, time will tell and he's plenty young enough just now." Tomo's heart sank. It was the same old story that he'd heard almost since he could remember and which had begun the day Jackie was born. Even though his contact with his father had been perfunctory and spasmodic, somehow Tomo had just never been quite good enough and here it was again; Jackie the golden wonder! He had hoped that things might change now that he'd proven himself a soldier and made come true his father's dream of having a son follow in his footsteps. But of course he'd forgotten about the J effect on everything in his life. Even J's current girlfriend had been engaged to him until J came home from University and gazumped him in love.

"Thank you Sir," he couldn't ever quite bring himself to call his father 'dad', "but I've accepted a posting into the 4th battalion, infantry." He hesitated, wondering whether to provide reasons for his decision, but swiftly decided that any justification that he might offer would be dismissed out of hand with absolutely no consideration of its validity. So what would be the point?

"Harrumph!" was the only response forthcoming.

Precisely forty minutes later, having drunk their tea and eaten, in utter silence, the dainty sandwiches, ridiculously inappropriate for two such sizeable men, Tomo rose to his feet. He firmly shook his father's hand and bringing his heels together with a sharp tap, saluted smartly. He turned abruptly and left the building. Once outside he breathed deeply, squared his shoulders and without looking back, quick-marched himself across the parade ground and, for the last time, to the barracks which he'd called home for too many days and weeks and months. His bag lay ready on his bed and swinging it up onto his back, he briefly checked the surfaces and floor for potentially forgotten items and with happy memories of harsh lessons, bonds of friendship and absolutely no regrets, he took the first step onto the next rung of the ladder of life.

***

Nobody noticed the single tear that trickled its way down the creases and wrinkles of the aging cheek. It was dismissed and brushed away by the back of a hand before it could reach the peninsula chin and drip onto the chest where it might stain the ceremonial uniform shirt. Harry also breathed deeply before taking his ancient pipe from his pocket. The ritual of tapping out the ash, re-filling the bowl, tamping it down, topping it up, holding a match to the rusty herb and drawing in that first lung of tobacco filled smoke, exhaling it slowly and deliberately, calmed his senses, stilled his emotions and allowed him to regain his composure as Sgt Harold Stanton, the martinet that everyone feared and secretly loved to hate.

Chapter Four

The pain was indescribably intense. She tried to ease the rubber carefully from her swollen calves without removing what remained of her chafed skin. Once she was down to her socks she paused, not relishing the idea of greater agonies, and considered her options. She could leave the socks on, perhaps convincing herself they would act as bandages, or she could peel them off and all her skin with them. Instead she hobbled across the back passage, leaving the offending mucky wellingtons splayed across the narrow access, and in through the unlocked kitchen door. The soft rustling sound of hooves in straw and heads in hay, emanating from the big barn which overshadowed the small tied cottage tucked tenuously on one end, dimmed to nothing more than the occasional breathy snort and clink of a halter chain punctuated with indignant clucks from the roosting chooks. As the door closed behind her, she reached for the kettle and slid it onto the already hot hob of the big black Aga stove she had stoked earlier. Realising the water would be hot already; she dragged the tin bath from its usual resting place under the kitchen table and slid it across the flagged floor to in front of the stove. Soon she was sipping a hot cup of tea as she, socks still on, reclined in the hot soapy bubbles and considered her current conundrum.

It was becoming increasing clear that she could not continue this way. Quite apart from the impossibility of managing everything single handed, there were just not enough hours in the day to carry out even the basic essentials of running the farm. And to cap it all the weather wasn't helping. Three weeks of continuous rain had taken its toll on the yard, the barn, the lane and even the higher meadows were waterlogged. She had to bring the cattle down to the home ground; that in itself being quite a task for one woman and her dog, and now the straw supplies and the grain were fast becoming scarce. What was she to do?

Later, having checked the barn once more and finding all quiet, having eaten a simple meal of bread and cheese and having tried to read another chapter of the novel in which she attempted to escape reality, she smeared her now bare legs; bare of skin as well as of the socks which had sloughed off easily in the bathwater, with ointment; cattle ointment since that was all she had available. Binding them with fresh strips of linen she made her painful way up the rickety stairs to the small mezzanine bedroom area. She instinctively looked across to the big four poster bed that filled most of the limited space. She still could not bring herself to sleep in the bed that had been their private heaven. Previously, she had slept downstairs in the single room which served as kitchen, diner and lounge. She had only moved her trundle bed up here after they were gone because here it was warmer at night since the decking floor was directly above the Aga and was thus heated via the chimney breast. They were not here anymore and she missed them. However, this was no time for self-pity and she had sworn to herself that she would not become overwhelmed by grief; there were the animals to care for and far greater financial issues to resolve. And she would do it better after a good night's sleep.

***

Windy Ridge Farm had once been a thriving establishment with both animal husbandry and arable production high enough to sustain the workers and the Manor house residents and staff. It wasn't particularly large in terms of acreage but it was rich and verdant with an abundance of small streams and rivulets which were not usually enough to cause the ground to become waterlogged but were plentiful enough to encourage growth and fodder for all. Although their meat production was small, just a few calves and piglets each year, mainly for their own consumption, their milk market was more than buoyant. The grain they produced was sold to the big cereal manufacturers in exchange for a regular supply of flours and cattle feed and Sally and her parents had often laughingly claimed that they were the British Breakfast providers for all of England. And it wasn't so very far from the truth.

The first blow to hit them had come with an outbreak of Foot and Mouth disease which brought with it the devastation of both the beef and the milk herds. And as if that wasn't enough, soon after a cold, hard winter there followed a long summer of drought which made for a very meagre grain crop and little hay or silage for the winter months. The once thriving farm became gradually more and more run down and parts of it almost derelict since no one had the motivation or money to rectify the problems. The big barn, originally filled to the rafters with hay and straw, with bins of cattle feed lining the walls and milk churns waiting for collection, was now home to the two aging farm horses, a few Jacobs sheep and, of course, the chickens. The small herd of milking cows was housed in what used to be the stables, next to the milking parlour and just a stone's throw from the pasture where they now grazed, weather permitting.

***

Sally sat sipping her morning coffee as she contemplated the state of her feet and legs. The wounds had seeped through her makeshift bandages, drying hard like a crust encased sausage. Should she try to remove them? Or perhaps it would be better to shove her legs, bandages and all, into the discarded wellingtons and try to forget the pain. She took the latter choice and a few moments later could be seen hobbling across the yard to see to the morning milking. The tanker would be here in an hour's time and there were a dozen cows to milk by hand before then. The generator blew last week and Sally had not had time to call out the electrician although, truth to tell, she rather liked milking by hand. She could nuzzle her head into the cow's warm flank and breathe in the sweet fresh smell of grass turned to milk. The animal's soft and regular breathing was soothing to her senses and she relaxed in the knowledge that she needn't think of anything else until this task was completed.

She had wanted, or rather needed, to plough the top meadow but it was unusually and thoroughly waterlogged and the two horses would not be able to pull the heavy machinery through the sticky muddy land. Instead she walked the creatures the mile or so up to the top of the lane and back in order to give them a little exercise, groomed them perfunctorily and fed them a quarter of the final bag of feed. She collected the very few eggs; well only three, but they would make her a meal and maybe a cake too. She fed the chooks and sheep before preparing to visit the solicitor in town. Any day this week at three in the afternoon he said. There was nothing else she had to do; only the numerous things that she couldn't actually physically do alone and so today was the day! Well it would take her an hour to walk there and it was already one thirty. There was just time to eat a piece of toast and cheese and then she must be on her way...

***

Gradually, strange sounds began to filter through the blackness which enveloped her in a cocoon of lightheaded comfort. She did not want to wake up and open her eyes but the insistent voice gave no ground for refusal. Reluctantly she turned her head towards the sound and opened one eye just enough to see a small golden blonde curly haired figure bobbing up and down beside her bed. Bed? What was she doing in bed and, come to think of it, where on earth was she? She struggled to make sense of her surroundings; listening to strange bleepings and distant muffled voices. There was an all pervading aroma of disinfectant lightly dusted with floral overtones and the ever present, although unappetising, whiff of food cooking somewhere nearby. Despite her best efforts she could not sit up. Something was weighing heavily on her legs and the rest of her felt too light and as if it didn't quite belong, like pieces of a jigsaw puzzle forced into the wrong places. She gave up the struggle and closing her eyes again whispered briefly, "Where am I and who are you?" The child beside her smiled broadly and traced his fingertip over the back of her idle hand where it lay limply on the bedcovers, "I'm Timothy!" he declared proudly, "and I'm six years old." There was a pause before he continued gravely, "I fink you are in hospital." Of course! Her eyes flew open again. Now she could make some sense of the sounds and smells. But why, how, where, when... the questions teemed in her head although she wasn't at all sure that this diminutive person could provide her with adequate answers. She thought of asking him to fetch a nurse or doctor, anyone who could explain her situation, but her eyelids were too heavy to remain open and sleep overcame her again as she drifted back into a drug induced comatose state which lasted well into the next day.

Chapter Five

Sandra's head hurt. She really hadn't wanted to raise it from the pillow this morning but the dire threats and warnings of serious recriminations should she fail to meet yet another deadline at college or indeed should she not attend the tutorials timetabled for her subject, meant that she had no choice in the matter. Thus it was that she stood shivering and feeling very sorry for herself, at the lonely bus stop outside the chandler's store. The wind was whipping up the waters beyond the harbour wall and the spume was flung over the ancient stonework which purported to shelter the small fishing village. For the millionth time she wondered how anyone could endure this Godforsaken place. She tugged at the scarf wound bandana style around her head, disguising the error of judgement she had made last night. She must remember to thank Tom properly when she next saw him. He had saved the day for her and she had been surprised by his unexpected kindness and quick thinking. Perhaps he wasn't such a geek after all?

Before too long, and just before she gave up on the anticipated bus's arrival, the old green coach trundled around the corner and ground to a creaking halt several yards short of the stop. Sandra gathered up her books and bag and hurried to climb the three short steps up into the relative warmth of the bus. It was surprisingly full today. Often she would be the only passenger until they reached the next village but today there were only a few empty seats. She sat down besides an austere looking, grey haired lady who seemed harmless enough and hopefully was unlikely to want to strike up a conversation. How wrong can one be?

"A good old-fashioned full English breakfast and plenty of water should have cured that you know." Her voice was light and sounded younger than she looked.

"Thanks," muttered Sandra before she had a chance to wonder how on earth the woman knew she had a hangover.

"We all do these things from time to time." the voice continued although the lady appeared to be gazing out of the window, "Just make sure you appreciate the experience and learn from it." Just who did she think she was? What gave this complete stranger the right to preach to her? Was she some sort of missionary sent to save wayward girls? Sandra turned her head to look more closely and was taken by surprise to find herself gazing into two piercingly blue unblinking eyes. Before she had time to react, a brilliant smile lit up the aging face making it appear much younger, and a hand shot out from within the cosy muff wherein it tried to preserve some semblance of warmth. "How do you do; I am Bethany."

Sandra took the hand and shook it perfunctorily in automatic response to the gesture. She hesitated before responding; after all what harm could there be in telling this stranger her name? "I'm Sandra, but my friends call me Sandy." Now why had she added that? This woman wasn't her friend at all. In fact she didn't even know the woman! She wasn't sure whether to continue with some trivial nicety but Bethany saved her the decision by delving into her capacious handbag. She withdrew a small bottle of some evil smelling potion a tiny drop of which she poured onto her forefinger before reaching out to touch Sandra's forehead. Sandra pulled back in surprise but not before the extended digit wiped a little of the stuff onto her skin. Immediately she began to feel better. The oppressive headache began to lift and her muscles began to ache less. "God man, what's in that stuff?" The words sprang out before she had time to consider to whom she spoke.

Bethany laughed; a bright tinkle of a laugh which peeled out through the bus causing everyone to smile at her obvious delight. "Well since I'm neither God nor a man, I don't think I feel obliged to tell you! Does it work?"

"It sure does! You could make a fortune with that stuff you know." In response Bethany simply smiled to herself and replaced the cap on the bottle before secreting it away in her bag once more.

The rest of the journey was spent in a comfortable silence. Despite the fact that Sandra would now have welcomed some conversation in order to alleviate the boredom of the hour and a half bus ride, she did not encourage Bethany to talk. She somehow knew that words were not needed in order to forge a strange sort of travelling companionship bond between them. They did no more than exchange the occasional glance and smile whilst retaining their own thoughts accompanied by the general hubbub of other people's muffled conversations.

***

It wasn't until much later, after lunch break if fact, that Sandra realised that she had unthinkingly removed the bandana from her head. No one had commented on her maimed fringe. Absolutely no one; not even her arch enemy, Carmen, who would have taken great delight in pointing out to everyone just how stupid Sandy looked with her stubby fringe! Quickly she pulled out her handbag mirror, hoping Mr McMarnie wouldn't see her, and glanced at her forehead. There, as usual, were the irritating curls that she thought she had clipped off. She had no time to examine her hair more closely for Mr McMarnie had indeed seen the mirror and his scathing comment made it quite clear that she was in trouble yet again.

***

The phone call came as no surprise. Of course she'd missed the bus home. She did it more often than not; although that was tempered with the fact that she did not bother to attend as often as she should. Nevertheless, she had sounded genuinely upset this time and so he dragged his leather jacket over his aching shoulders and slid his feet back into the boots waiting by the door. He took his helmet and another from the shelf and the keys from the hook. A few moments later, he kick-started the big bike and headed off into town. It shouldn't take him more than twenty minutes to get there provided he didn't meet the inevitable herd of cattle being brought down for milking. One of the unexpected hazards he had learned to accept as the norm in this wild place.

Tom enjoyed his bike. It was one of his few pleasures up here where there were not many other vehicles to inhibit his freedom to swerve and slide round the ever winding lanes and race across the moors. Of course, when there were obstacles they were always big ones, such as slow moving farm machinery or very large herds of cattle, and often meant major delays or finding devious detours but by this forced means Tom was now pretty familiar with the geography in this locality.

Precisely twenty minutes later, after only one minor detour, he saw her sitting dejectedly on the steps outside the bus station. Wordlessly he handed her the helmet which she crammed onto her head over the recently replaced bandana, and buckled it securely. Unceremoniously she lifted her long flowing bohemian style skirts and flung her stockinged leg over the bike. Swiftly rearranging her clothing, tucking under her thighs the voluminous fabric and ensuring that her bag was securely over her shoulder, she shoved her hands into Tom's jacket pockets where they would both keep warmer and provide her with a steady grip when they swooped and swerved as she knew they would. Not for the first time had Tom come to her rescue and at last she was beginning to appreciate the value of having him around as opposed to the nuisance of having had to give up some of her space to him! She hugged him perhaps a little tighter than she had previously been inclined.

Chapter Six

The long, windswept and rocky path rose before her as she battled her way against the harsh elements, determined to reach her destination before nightfall. Elsa grimaced to herself as she pushed back under her hood an escapee strand of hair that threatened to painfully whip her face. She found herself wondering that she could never remember coming to this place in anything other than harsh conditions. Not that she'd been here often but visits to Old Bess always coincided with the need for understanding and guidance in some issue or other. Rarely, if ever, had she called for a social visit. Nevertheless, the old lady always welcomed her as a long lost friend and there was never any doubt of her genuine pleasure in Elsa's company.

After partaking of the usual array of freshly baked cakes and pastries of which there always seemed to be an endless supply, all washed down with an aromatic cup of herbal tea, Old Bess led Elsa through into the parlour. Sweeping the motley collection of cats from their various resting places, she pulled a second chair closer to the fire and invited Elsa to be seated and comfortable. She did not waste time on pleasantries, after all there was little she did not already know, but came straight to the point, "Tell me what the problem is my dear." Her open manner and compelling eyes demanded an equally forthright response from her audience and Elsa reacted accordingly. "Timothy," she said. There was a brief silence before Old Bess began to shake and then to roar with laughter. At first Elsa was taken aback but soon the infectious mirth had her smiling broadly and enjoying the sight of Old Bess rocking and crying with merriment.

"Why is it that the mere mention of his name can cause such hilarity?" The question rode on the back of her having witnessed Eleanor and Rosa's mirth at the mention of this particular moniker.

"Oh my dear," responded Bess as she dried her eyes on the corners of her voluminous apron, "if only you knew...!" It was clear that no explanation was to be forthcoming on this occasion since Old Bess rearranged her face into a suitable expression of seriousness and concern as she leant forward to touch Elsa's knee in reassurance of her renewed composure and compassion.

Suddenly, Elsa was unsure as to why she had sought out this venerable old lady. How to put into words the things that had begun to evidence themselves; little things that no one else might notice, such as the long conversations that Timothy appeared to have with an apparently invisible companion, his propensity for his own company and the long hours that he spent absorbed in some seemingly meaningless activity. And above all, the times, fleeting and yet significant, when he appeared to be completely absent, his body still and his eyes vacant, almost as though he was no longer living... Perhaps he was no different from any other child, and yet...

"It doesn't sound silly at all." Bess interrupted her thoughts and she looked up in surprise since she hadn't uttered anything of what was in her mind. "Come with me." The command brooked no refusal and so it was that Elsa found herself wrapped in a warm cloak and standing in the partially sheltered small back yard which overlooked the grey and uninviting waters far below. Beside her Old Bess, similarly clad, wound a rusty crank handle and an equally old and creaking bucket edged its way to the rim of the stone well over which they looked. Grunting a little with the effort, the old lady unhooked the handle of the bucketful of sparklingly fresh water and safely tied off the rope to a fitted cleat at the side of the well. Turning again to the well, she pulled her hood over her head and invited Elsa to do the same, thus creating a shadow through which better to see into the well below.

"Don't think, just look," said the venerable old woman.

Despite her total trust in this sage who had been her guide and guardian for as long as she could remember, Elsa was puzzled as to what she was being shown. Nevertheless, and somewhat to her surprise, she found herself looking down into the inky blackness and gradually, as the dank murkiness of the well cleared and was apparently suffused with sunlight, she gazed upon a very familiar scene. There was Timothy, playing as usual in the muddy banks of the small stream that ran through the meadow behind the house. His golden hair and rosy cheeks shone with health and happiness as he, totally oblivious to his surroundings, focused solely on his game. The plastic soldiers with which he played lay scattered in seemingly random patterns on the wet ground. There was none of the more usual guttural and plosive noises made by young boys at war play or shooting games, he played in a silence within which there was no doubt of communication since he acted and reacted in such a way that it was obvious he was not the only player in this game.

As she watched, the scene began to dissolve and change. A sound of gunfire startled her and that, combined with an acrid smell which invaded her senses, caused her to instinctively draw back from the well. "What is happening?" She silently questioned, but Old Bess shook her head and indicated that she should look again. Elsa did so and was surprised to see a darkened scene, hazy with unidentifiable swirling smoke and mists, strange lights sweeping across the skies and in the bottom left hand corner, a small figure with bright blond though tousled hair, lying face down and apparently fast asleep on the edge of a muddy puddle. An involuntary gasp and Elsa looked up again into the gently smiling and reassuring face of her mentor. "Come inside." Though brief, her words were comforting and Elsa withdrew the hood from her hair and shook her head to clear the teeming questions that threatened to occlude all sensible thought. She remembered well an earlier lesson; trust your intuition, don't interfere, let things happen, and her faith in this mantra, combined with her trust in Old Bess helped her to know that she was being allowed to understand something more profound than she had previously experienced.

She had always known that there was something very special and indecipherable about Old Bess. She was never quite sure how she came to know her nor from whence her knowing had come. She could clearly remember being here as a small child but she could neither remember who brought her nor however she left. Nevertheless, not only did she function elsewhere in the world, Elsa also had inexplicable memories of a past which, had she tried to explain it to ordinary folks, would sound fantastical, improbable and downright crazy. Thus it was she never mentioned these things but kept them close to her heart. She was intuitive and perceptive and understood without being told that her purpose was to facilitate the purposes of others and to guide them as best she could into making good choices as they found their way through the paths and jungles of life's chaotic courses.

Old Bess took her hand as they sat facing each other in the big armchairs either side of the glowing fire, "There are things you should know about this little boy and now is the time to begin…"

Chapter Seven

"Tomo! Tomo!" Shell shocked and deafened by the thunderous explosions that had now mercifully ceased, Tomo could not hear the words he saw mouthed by the frightened and grubby face that leant over him. The face gave a shout, again unheard by the prostrate Tomo, and faded from his sight. He began gingerly to feel his various limbs, testing for movement in the further extremities of his body. His left leg hurt and gradually he realised that it was lying at an extraordinary angle, that there was no feeling in his foot and that it was almost certainly broken. Blood oozed from the impossibly dirty fabric of his trouser leg and began to colour in the yellowy mud of the puddle in which he lay. He watched disinterestedly as the puddle gradually turned orangey brown and he even admired the swirling mix of colours the blood, mud and oil created. He felt no pain except when he tried to move. Accordingly he kept still, content, for the time being, to wait for someone to come to help him. For some strange reason the words "any port in a storm" kept resounding in his head. 'How incongruous!' he thought, 'for this is not a port and I don't remember there being a storm.' His mind continued to wander disjointedly, as if he were caught in some impossible dream and he drifted in and out of consciousness until the concerned face reappeared. This time accompanied by two other vague figures, indistinguishable in their filthiness, but identifiable by the tattered Red Cross on the bag one of them carried. He knew they were talking to him and about him but no sounds emanated from their mouths and as they gently lifted him onto a stretcher, he gave up the struggle and sank into a merciful oblivion.

It was some time later that he became aware of muffled sounds and a clinical antiseptic aroma mingled with the all-pervasive smell of unwashed bodies and filth. Although he attempted to open his eyes he could see no more than minor variations in the darkness; paler greens contrasted with khaki all around him and the blackness of a night sky, dotted with an occasional bright star, peeked through the gaps in the canvas roof over his head. It was oppressively hot under the heavy cloth that lay across his chest and he tried to lift his arm to push back the covering. However, his arm was tethered to a makeshift pole and a fine tube led from the plastic liquid filled bag, suspended from its uppermost point, to a needle inserted in the inside of his elbow joint. He turned his head slightly to peer more closely at the contraption and was startled to see a small boy standing at his bedside and gazing at him expressionlessly. The solemn child mouthed a single word but again the sound was unheard by Tomo's damaged auditory orifices. Shivering despite the heat in his torso, he found he could not control the tremble of his limbs nor could he keep his eyelids from closing as the inexorable heaviness and dull witted clouding of his mind insisted on his drifting into the morphine induced haze that cocooned him from the reality of his apparently inexplicable situation. Where was the fighting? Where were his men? And where exactly was he? Although answers would perhaps have provided some small comfort, in reality he was not in the slightest concerned about these or any other matters. Resisting no more, he slept the sleep of the innocent and the anaesthetised.

The pain hit him like a ton of bricks falling onto his legs. His left leg took the brunt of the metaphorical weight and he cried out in agony as he found himself abruptly wide awake and with all his senses amplified. All that is except his auditory faculty which remained stubbornly muffled, although somewhat repaired from its earlier total absence. He gradually became aware of a green clad figure leaning over him, taking his pulse, wiping his brow and finally injecting some substance into his arm via the cannula that restricted the movement of his elbow. The torture in his leg subsided as the morphine spread through his body and before long his eyes closed again; but not before he had caught a glimpse of the same small boy, crowned with a shock of honey blonde curls, standing incongruously in the corner of the room and gazing solemnly and expressionlessly at the prostrate figure on the bed. Whos and whys and whats flitted through his already clouded mind before they disappeared into the ether of his drug enhanced sleep.

Much later, it seemed, he was woken again. This time he recognised the gruff, albeit muffled, voice of his senior officer and it wasn't until he heard a second voice respond to the indistinguishable enquiry that he realised with a start that his hearing had partially returned. Sounds were still muddied and words indecipherable but he was reassured by the comforting sounds of other voices. Officer Grant came over to his bedside and placed an envelope on the cage that covered Tomo's legs. "They're flying you out of here young man." Grant announced, "You've got a ticket back to Old Blighty. So long soldier and best of luck old man." As he turned from the bed he shook his head as he muttered, "You're going to need it mate."

There was no time to reflect on reasons or rationale and in any case none of this made any sense to him. As though drifting through some sort of nightmare, he did not resist and apart from the reality of the pain, everything else was surreal and inexplicable. Before he could close his eyes again, two more green clad men came and lifted his stretcher from the makeshift bed and carried him, still attached to the medical equipment, out to a waiting helicopter. Irrespective of the amount of care the two orderlies took and in automatic response to the unexpected movement, indescribable pain shot through his leg and he was grateful for the merciful relief that a second injection of morphine gave him. The whirring of the rotor blades became his lullaby as he gave way to the insistent heaviness of his eyelids…

**

Elsa's eyelids began to droop as the warmth of the fire and the soothing monotone of Old Bess's aging voice created a cocoon of soporific security which was lulling her to sleep. Realising the situation and Elsa's need for rest, Bess ceased her soliloquy and bustled round, shooing the numerous cats from under her feet, and produced a warm drink for her guest, whilst also preparing a comfortable bed in the corner of the room, nearest to the fireplace.

Elsa gratefully sipped the drink and pondered on the things she had learned thus far. Some of it was almost beyond comprehension and she struggled to make sense of the overall pattern that was emerging from the series of events her mentor described. However, there was a vital piece missing from the puzzle and she knew that she must wait patiently until Old Bess was ready to tell her more.

Soon she was tucked up in the cosy corner and drifted peacefully off into the land of dreams and spirits.

***

All around her was water. As far as she could see the shallow lake, dotted with clumps of sedge grasses and rushes, spread further, much further than she could ever remember seeing it before. In summer time it would be dry and carpeted with soft springy grass and delicate meadow flowers, but for now it was wet. She searched for him with her eyes and her heart. Her soul was calling to his; a thin reedy whisper on the invisible breeze, she imagined she could see it, a trail of vapour like fairy dust which swirled and chased after the cry. She slid her feet carefully over the sodden grasses, feeling for firm footholds in the muddy earth below and not wishing to disturb the surface of this veritable sea which spread before her. Again she called him and again her eyes raked the horizon, straining for a glimpse of movement or flash of light to show her where he was.

She felt no real concern and nothing about it seemed particularly strange. She certainly wasn't frightened and neither was she entirely comfortable since she knew that there was something she must do, find, protect and, above all, teach. Teach what she knew not but it was of no importance. In the distance she saw a slight flurry and heard a slight splash followed by a tinkling laugh. She hurried as carefully as she could toward the place from whence the disturbance had emanated but her progress was hampered by the long skirts that wrapped themselves wetly around her legs and threatened to make her trip and fall headlong into the still water. Straining her eyes to see whatever else might manifest itself she struggled to follow her spirit and find this enigmatic prey. She, the hunter, knew he was there and that was enough. Sooner or later she would find him and take him into her arms once more; holding his slight body close and feeling the energy in him combine with hers whilst they danced together. And so it was, in the timelessness of her dream, they came together and she held him whilst he smiled up into her eyes. "I found him," he said as he held up for her inspection a model toy soldier. The green and brown painted plastic was muddy and a little twisted with the head bent forward and one leg almost severed at the knee but the soldier still held his rifle and on his face was moulded the fiercely fixed smile that told of courage, honour and patriotism.

"Well done," she breathed into his hair...

Chapter Eight

The pool of muddy gravel at the bottom grated deliciously against his pink skin. He ran his fingers through the sludge and slid it carefully up the side of the tub. Carefully he made patterns; swirls, wriggles and lines, on the shiny enamel surface, admiring their changing shapes as they drifted back down into the soapy water. Splashing merrily he rinsed away the remaining specs before submerging himself completely and burying his nose in the soupy mess below. He wriggled his body like a seal and pushed himself along the length of the bath before emerging, bedraggled and on his nose a smudge of brown, to leap out over the side into the waiting fluffy towel held in the arms of his beloved 'sister'.

Carrie laughed at him as he squirmed out of her arms and ran to the small bowl balanced on the windowsill. In it lay a toy soldier, clean, although resting on a miniature bed of muddy sludge, but a little mangled and damaged. Carefully Timothy lifted the soldier out onto a flannel; an enormously too big towel for such a tiny figure, and dried it. He held it out for Carrie to see, "Broken, see?" and she took it from him.

"Unca Shane fix it," she said and placed it in her pocket.

A very short while later one head of blond curls was buried in a soft pillow as the child slept and clasped in his hand was the small drilled pebble that had resided in a polished box on his bedside table. A golden pebble, hung from a silver chain, and just about the size of his thumb, smooth and even surfaced, it rested snugly in his small palm.

***

"But what was he doing?" the exasperated question came again.

38

"My not know Wosa." Carrie was becoming frustrated in her attempt to explain how she had lost Timothy late that afternoon, how she had gone out alone to find him. How Shane had found her; crying and frightened, and how Elsa had brought Timothy home. He was covered from head to toe in muddy water and grime. He had lost a shoe and was wearing only a pair of shorts and a light shirt. In his hand was the toy and on his face was the delighted smile of a trophy winner. No one, it seemed, had a plausible explanation, not even Timothy himself. His version of events started and stopped with his finding of the all-important soldier. Carrie explained that she had stopped to look at a butterfly on a leaf and in that split second Timothy had simply disappeared. There was nowhere for him to hide and nothing to hide him from her but he was nowhere in sight, nor was there any sound from him or any other thing.

Rosa was justifiably concerned. Should she have left Timothy in Carrie's care? He was so much more difficult to keep tabs on these days. School had given him a confidence that he had previously lacked and he wandered further and further from the meadow in his solo games. Still preferring his own company to that of his peers or elders, Timothy was often to be found engrossed in some imagined dynasty or other world. His favourite toys were the band of soldiers that were never far from his side. He did not appear to use them to fight battles and preferred peaceable games wherein the soldiers helped each other and built bridges and mud huts in which to live. Sometime, however, they were obliged to defend their developments. Perhaps an army of ants would march through their land or perhaps a giant earthworm would flatten their fragile homes. Then a fierce battle would ensue, but without casualties on either side, the danger would be removed and the re-ordered game continued.

Perhaps, had Elsa not been visiting her aunt for those two days, this might not have happened. Isn't it always the case that when one thing changes then other things change accordingly? Rosa gazed from the window as the rain continued to pour down, the blackness outside showing her nothing more than the drops gliding down the glass pane and her own reflection appearing to melt in the wetness. She sighed again and turned from her pondering. She smiled at Carrie, "Come here Sweetness," she held out her arms to the tentative girl, "I know you did your best and he's home safe and sound now. We must just remember to be a little more careful another time." Carrie nestled into her adoptive stepmother's chest and squeezed her tight as she mumbled, "Fank oo Wosa."

Shane bounced into the room, "Got him squeaky clean again?" he enquired but before anyone answered him he roared with laughter, "My God that boy will be the death of us! Did you see the state of him?" His enjoyment of the child's escapade released the tension in the room and soon all were chuckling or laughing at the exploits of the sometimes strange and wayward boy.

Elsa sat quietly in the corner. Not only was she trying not to feel too irresponsible for taking a short break from her duties, but she was also trying to come to terms with the odd similarity between her dream and the events that unfolded on her return. There were differences of course, the meadow is not flooded and she found him by chance rather than by looking for him. Just as she had rounded the corner in the lane, before turning to cross the bridge over the stream that bordered the grounds of Willow Lodge, she had heard a triumphant yell. Startled she glanced quickly in the direction from which the sound had come, just in time to see Timothy emerge from the stream, completely saturated and plastered with mud. The rest we know; Shane had arrived back with sobbing Carrie just a few minutes before she hurried through the door half carrying the by now shivering child.

Despite her long dialogue with Old Bess there were still things she did not fully understand and yet she knew that much of it she had to learn and experience for herself. Notwithstanding, there were things that she instinctively knew and sometimes when she opened her mind and heart, she knew that there was something a little different about her life and that of those around her. Similarly there was something about Timothy; a connection that could not be explained through flesh and blood, and she was here to guide him.

***

"Shane," Carrie halted as she began to leave the room, "look!" she demanded. She held out the broken soldier and her brother took it carefully from her palm.

"Oo fix it?" she asked.

"I'll have a go Old thing," he replied, "Not sure I can save the leg but I'll see what I can do." Once again the soldier was buried deep in a pocket wherein it remained until several days later when Shane remembered and took it down to his workshop to inspect for damage and possible repair strategies.

***

Somewhere far away, in the blackness of his own closed eyelids, a soldier listened to the unfamiliar muffled sounds and voices that gently penetrated the unconsciousness of his mind. Now he was definitely awake but still the blackness persisted. He made a small movement and instantly it seemed a white and blue clad nurse was at his bedside, taking his wrist to feel his pulse and touching the back of her hand against his forehead. "Are you with us again now?" a gentle voice enquired and he began to nod his head. A fierce pain shot down his spine and into his left leg and an involuntary moan escaped his lips. "Lie still." The same gentle voice accompanied by a hand pressing him carefully back onto the pillows, "There was some damage to your ears and you must keep still while they heal." The explanation was far from reassuring and whilst it didn't really make sense of the pain in his spine and leg, it did explain the bandage wrapped around his head and which had slipped low over his eyes, thus causing the temporary blindness with which he appeared to be afflicted.

Noticing his predicament the gentle hands eased the bandage upward and he found himself looking into the intensely blue eyes of a matronly woman. She smiled kindly at him and introduced herself as Nurse Isabella, "your primary carer for the time being. Anything you want or need please ask me and I'll do my best to help you." However, for the time being he couldn't think of anything to ask for other than an explanation of where he was and how he came to be there. Even for this information, he couldn't be bothered to ask for his eyes were beginning to close again, almost as though the effort to take in anything other than the bed he lay on was simply too much.

A little later, he was aware of other people coming and going; doctors he presumed, and nurses, and the ever presence of the motherly lady who was watching over him. The bandage over his ears was carefully removed and the dressing replaced this time with sticky tape and no prohibitive bandage. A large cage held the blankets off his lower body and someone peered beneath in such a way as he could not have seen even had he felt it necessary to try. But he was content to let these people fuss around him. He floated in and out of a drug induced dreamless sleep which enveloped him in its emptiness.

Chapter Nine

By the fifth day she was able, propped by many pillows, to sit up and survey her unfamiliar surroundings. Nurse Liza had explained to her that she had been brought into A&E last Tuesday. She had been found by a lady who, whilst walking her dog, had found Sally collapsed and lying, unconscious, in a ditch. The kind soul had raised the alarm and had even accompanied Sally, a complete stranger, to the hospital. Nurse Liza went on to tell her how the damage to her legs had become septic and that the poison had worked its way quickly through her blood because of the energetic pumping of her heart whilst she was briskly walking to her appointment with the solicitor.

One week later and Sally was on her way home. When Sally announced that she would go home by bus, Nurse Liza insisted on ordering and paying for a taxi to take her right to her front door. "It really wouldn't be wise to walk the half mile up your driveway!" she cautioned. She smiled at Sally and held out a slip of paper, "This is the name of the lady who helped you. I thought you might like to contact her when you feel stronger." Sally was humbled that she had not thought to ask the name of her saviour but her sorrow was short lived since Liza continued, "She asked me not to tell you but... well I've done it now so it's up to you whether you choose to try to find her. I'm afraid she gave only her first name and a sketchy address, no town or other details."
"Thank you." was all Sally could utter as she brushed a tear aside with one hand and pushed the scrap of paper into her coat pocket with the other. She wrapped her arms around the nurse and they held each other close for a warm second or two in a brief meeting of hearts, minds and mutual understanding.

***

So worried was she about what she would find on her return home that she hurried from the car to her front door, studiously ignoring the urge to look across the darkening farmyard. Thus it was that on her arrival, she failed to notice. Having thanked the driver for carrying her bag into the house, she closed the front door and drank in the peace and isolation that she had so craved in that noisy, overly warm and stifling place she had so recently left. Although it was still only early evening, she made herself a warm drink and clambered carefully up the stairs. Glancing briefly at the untidy heap of bedding strewn over her own bed and realising she was ready at last, she crossed to the big four poster bed. Shrugging off her overcoat and shoes, she slipped under the duvet and relaxed as warmth spread through her and, for the first time since she emerged from her drug induced semi-comatose state, she slept soundly.

***

The crowing of the cock woke her early next morning. Only for a brief moment did she wonder where she was and as the memory emerged, she stretched luxuriously and felt a deep contentment within.

Before long she was carefully easing her still sore legs into a new pair of well-padded wellingtons. It did not occur to her to wonder from whence they had come. There they were, waiting for her feet and so she wore them. She made her way across the yard to the cattle shed. She was amazed to see that the cattle were already tethered in the milking parlour and the gentle hum of the milking machine told of a repair to the generator. As though in a dream, she turned and looked back through the wide flung doors and into the old barn. Neatly arranged on one side were feed bags and bales of straw. On the other were the two well-groomed work horses. Wonderingly, Sally made her way up the lane toward the top field. This time she was not surprised to see that it was ploughed over and resting, ready for the spring planting of next year's harvest. She did not understand how or who, but someone had taken good care of the farm in her absence.

Increasingly painfully, she made her way back to the farmhouse. Imagine her surprise when she found in her kitchen area, a smiling friendly woman who welcomed her in as though she were the hostess and Sally the guest. "You must be tired!" she fussed, "You really shouldn't be up and about too quickly you know. You've been very ill!" Sally sat down abruptly; eloquently proving the point made, and gratefully accepted the proffered mug of steaming coffee. This was followed by a light breakfast; a boiled egg with toast and marmalade. Soon the good food was making Sally sleepy and she made her way across the living space to the saggy old sofa. Before long she was lying comfortably tucked under a fleecy blanket with her head pillowed on a velvety cushion. Sleep overcame her for a while until she was woken by the sound of voices and the clink of cutlery on crockery. There was a delicious smell of fresh baked bread and some rich meaty meal. Sally realised she felt truly hungry for the first time in a long time!

"Come and join us my dear." The kindly woman came and took her arm to assist her to the table. "It's time we introduced ourselves anyway. And I think we may have some explaining to do too."

"Thank you," Sally whispered weakly, "I'm Sally. I live here," she said, somewhat incredulously and with a questioning lilt, demonstrating her lack of comprehension. The response was a rumble of laughter from the round belly of the big man who sat in her father's place at the table. He was nothing like her father who had been a short, wiry though strong man who rarely laughed but who had a heart of gold. This man, who occupied her father's place, was wrinkled with laugh lines. With greying, long ringlet strands of curly hair and a whiskery beard, he emanated warmth and good humour. His hands, with calluses and scars in the roughened skin, his nails short and scrubbed clean, bore witness to his being a working man.

"Well, young lady," he began while Sally blushed at the unexpected compliment. Young? She hadn't been that for a long time! He continued, "You gave everyone quite a scare now didn't you?" Sally nodded briefly and was about to ask when he spoke again. "It looks to me as though this had been building up for some time. The place was in a bit of a shambles wasn't it?" again she nodded, "Well thank goodness we got wind of your predicament and came along in time to sort you out." Sally was totally bewildered. Who were these people and how did they come to know so much about her and her situation?

"Now, now Daniel," chided the woman, "You haven't even told her your name yet." And then she too laughed aloud as she realised her unintentional joke. "Oh my but that's a good one," she chortled as she wiped her eyes on the edge of her apron. As soon as she had composed herself she began again, "I'm Dora and this is Daniel. We're very pleased to meet you at last."

"Pleased to meet you too and astonished at all that you seem to have done." Sally didn't know where to begin thanking these people, their kindness and hard work seemed limitless. She was mentally trying to frame her questions into sensible sentences when Dora broke in again, "I'm sure you have many questions for us but now is not the time to answer them all. The first thing is for you to know that we are here to help you for as long as you need us. You're not to worry about money or managing the farm or anything else, it is all taken care of, and what you must do is get properly well so that we can look to the future and make some changes."

Dora brooked no argument and so it was, a short time later, that Sally, utterly overwhelmed, found herself once more tucked up on the sofa with the ubiquitous romantic novel in her hand but with her eyes turned inward and her mind occupied with trying to make sense of it all…

***

"My want a moo cows and a sheepsies an' a t'actor. Please mummy, please mummy." The unusual insistence with which he pleaded spurred Rosa into conceding to his request. Later that afternoon, following a trip to the little village toy store, young Timothy was to be found playing in the sand pit with a small collection of plastic farm animals, a fork and some cardboard boxes. Gradually he turned the gleaming white sand into some semblance of a small farm. He placed the boxes to form a farmhouse and barns. With the fork handle he drew a road leading to the farmyard; he sprinkled grass for fields and gravel for paths, he 'ploughed' a field of mud with the prongs of the fork and he gathered up sticks and leaves to create hedgerows and fences. Taking the clay from the bottom of the muddy puddles, he copied the shapes of his plastic prizes and made more clumsy cows, pigs and sheep and even smaller specks of shapes that might have been chickens. Soon his fields were full and the smile on his face bore witness to the pleasures a few plastic farm animals and a large dollop of imagination can supply to a small child.

Chapter Ten

The rain continued to flood the earth and fill, with treacherous results, the pot holes in the roads. And so it was with only minor regret that Tom glanced at the tarpaulin covered bike where it stood chained to the iron fence which divided his Uncle's property from the neighbouring front yard. Pulling his collar up around his chin, tugging his sou'-wester far down over his eyes and shoving his hands deep into his pockets, Tom made his way along the harbour wall to the rickety bus shelter near the Post Office.

How was he going to tell her? Both of them, and within just a few days, it seemed impossible, rather like something out of a film, and so unreal that he felt he was living in some sort of nightmare. She would already be annoyed that the bike was unrepaired and going home by bus would not meet with any sort of enthusiasm. Perhaps he should hire a taxi? But the few small coins in his pocket would not stretch to that and his credit card was used to the hilt. Even just these last few days, whilst he tried to deal with the ensuing chaos, had eaten up the remains of his savings. He sighed deeply and, not for the first time, wondered why these things seem to continually happen to him. Wasn't it enough that the vehicle coming the other way had caused him to swerve? And why wasn't she holding on to him as she usually did? Of course it would have to have been a police car and the inevitable paperwork had been headache enough, but on top of that he had this overwhelming feeling of guilt to contend with.

Sandra sat in the hospital foyer, waiting for him to take her home. She knew she had taken advantage of his kind nature and she was ashamed although, at the same time, she couldn't suppress the little bubble of excitement that threatened to escape her in a giggle. Perhaps she could wind him around her little finger after all. She checked her appearance once more in the little compact mirror from her bag. She ran her finger sensuously across her lips and wondered what it might feel like to be kissed by him.

She knew he hadn't meant to tip her off the pillion seat and yet she had sworn at him mightily, calling him all sorts of unimaginably rude names. And it had hurt! Nothing broken but concussion, grazes, bruises and cuts to her hips, knees and shoulders had been extensive and her determination not to cry had resulted in her fury at him. All completely undeserved of course; he had been kindness itself and had stayed with her long after it was absolutely necessary. He had brought her clothes and toiletries from home and had visited her as often as possible whilst her wounds healed and her hair grew. That, it seemed, was the only major advantage of enforced captivity for a week or so! Such a mystery! The mirror, in school; the unintentional root of this enforced captivity, had definitely reflected her usual curly fringe, but when she had arrived here she saw only the hacked stubble that was the result of her former stupidity. At least now she could be free of that horrible, if genius, bandana and show her head in public again and without embarrassment.

Her stomach gave an involuntary flutter as he came striding into the neat, clinical hospital, and she stood up to greet him. She failed to notice the tightness of his expression and the taut control of his deportment. He nodded at her perfunctorily and took her bag from where it rested on the floor beside her chair. "You OK?" was all he said and she mumbled, "Ok" in assent.

"Where's the bike?" she asked, noticing that he was neither carrying his helmet, nor hers.

"Not fixed yet. I came on the bus."

"The bus!" she cried in horror, and a groan escaped her lips. He stopped and turned. He scrutinised her face and on seeing the remnants of the bruising around her cheek and chin, he took pity on her. "Come on I'll buy you a coffee, then we can try to find a taxi home." How on earth he was going to pay for it he really didn't know.

As it happened, he needn't have worried. The taxi driver turned out to be a friend of his Aunt and Uncle and, knowing what had befallen the unfortunate family, he waived any fare for taking them home. "My shout," he gruffly insisted. Nevertheless, Tom was wary, "Please don't say anything," he muttered to the man as they clambered into the vehicle, "she doesn't know yet."

"Know what?" her ears were sharper than he realised but he delayed telling her by dismissively ignoring her query. They sat in a reasonably comfortable silence all the way home although there was a tension between them and each knew there were things that the other needed to address. She wanted to move closer to him, to put her hand in his, or to lay her head on his shoulder. But historically they were not close and she did not know how to bring about the change that she thought she wanted. Her usually abrasive manner came to the fore and she wrapped around herself the protection of discontented youth and staying as distant as she was, she adopted a pouting sulky expression behind which to hide her newfound romantic interest in this enigmatic cousin of hers.

***

It can't be true! This isn't real. You're playing a joke on me. Aren't you? Sandra's uncomprehending mind teemed with possibilities. Anything rather than accept the truth her ears were hearing. Dead? Both of them? But how, why, what had happened…? There were no tears; simply incredulity and disbelief.

Patiently he explained: Aunt Aggie had been sick with a nasty chesty cold; her usual dose of winter bronchitis, and Uncle Joe had been out seeing to the lobster pots. It was somewhat later than usual since he, Tom, had been visiting Sandra and had not had time to do his usual chores. Especially since the bus times were erratic to say the least. The weather was wild, the seas high and although the tide was low, a rogue wave had tipped Joe over and rolled him in the cold, muddy shallows. He banged his head on a rock and knocked himself unconscious for a few minutes. A fellow fisherman scooped him up and took him to the lifeguard post on the end of the harbour and it was there that Aggie found him when a small boy was sent on an errand to fetch her. She really should not have left the house in the wild and wet, not with such a terrible fever, but her husband needed her and nothing and no one would have stopped her from going to him.

Realising that his injuries were slight, too slight to explain the degree of his current malady, she asked the Lifeguards to summons an ambulance which duly arrived and took not only him but her as well to the local cottage hospital. Not the big industrial place that was temporary home to Sandra, but somewhere much more homely if understaffed and ill equipped.

There was little they could do. Joe had suffered a cataclysmic stroke, possibly coincidentally but equally plausible as a result of the blow to his head and Aggie had developed pneumonia which, in her already weakened state, had insidiously hurried her demise. Within three days of each other, both were dead. Untimely yes, but both were well into their late sixties; an age after which death tends to lean over shoulders at all times, and both had enjoyed a good life in spite of their latter hardships. It was the unanticipated suddenness of it and the shock that hit them all so hard. In the blink of an eye, everything had been turned upside down, emphasising the fragility of this existence and demonstrating how easily sparks of life can be extinguished. Tom tried to comfort his cousin with the suggestion that neither of her parents would have wanted to go on living without the other. Inseparable in life they remained together in death.

***

It was at the funeral that he first saw him. A diminutive, golden haired boy with bright blue eyes, he was standing near the front of the crematorium chapel during the simple service with which the bodies were ushered out of this world. His solemn face and unblinking eyes were remarkable and for a split second Tom's gaze met his and it seemed their minds connected in mutual recognition. Nevertheless,

51

the moment was soon forgotten in the business of thanking guests, accepting muttered and often insincere, sympathetic comments, shaking hands and patting shoulders. Therefore, it wasn't until later that he was reminded of the incident. Tom remembered that the child had been holding a rose. Much to his astonishment, when he went to bed later that night, there on his pillow was the same single white rose, pearly iridescence, perfectly formed, exquisitely perfumed and nestled at its heart, a solitary diamond dewdrop. How it came to be there, he had no idea, but there it was and he took it up carefully and placed it in a tooth mug of water before shrugging his way under the duvet and allowing exhaustion to weigh down his eyelids and switch off all conscious thought.

Chapter Eleven

The unlikely duo stood side by side and stared dismally out at the incessant rain as it streamed down the window pane, dripped from the bowed down boughs of the heavily leaved trees and generally soaked the already sodden earth below. Too bad, too bad. Neither boy spoke and yet each knew the others' thoughts and both were unsure as to whether they felt sorrier for themselves or for the other. It really did seem grossly unfair that the two of them were stuck here, isolated to all intents and purposes, and denied the freedom and, for one at least, dubious pleasures of home and holidays.

***

It was Thomas who had found him that first time; large lumbering Thomas whose pale eyes, white hair and pallid skin looked incongruous on his swollen, almost obese, body. Not only was he tall for his age but he was unusually large, or well-built as his simple and over-indulgent mother insisted, and his habitual clumsiness accentuated his physical disadvantage. He had run, as best he could, to fetch matron who had clucked and fussed over the prone figure lying on the cloakroom floor. Mr Stamp, the site manager, had been summoned to carry the slight boy to sick bay and had deposited him unceremoniously and with a grunt of exertion, on the thin-mattressed iron bed before ushering Thomas out and to the headmaster's office to report the incident as accurately as possible.

Thomas was frightened. He had only just made friends with this newcomer and now it seemed as though he might die! His large pale eyes were orbs of fear and his hands shook a little as he opened the dreaded door to face the 'dragon' within.

"Come in, come in boy," commanded the imperious voice and Thomas stumbled through the old oak door as he caught his toes on the scuffed and almost threadbare carpet. "Careful son, we don't want another casualty just now do we?" Fred Barker smiled at the worried child, "Sit down over here and we'll have some tea and a chat."

Gradually Thomas began to relax and before long he was actually smiling as he realised this 'dragon' was really rather nice and much more like a bear cub; playful, humorous and soft, although Thomas was never in any doubt as to the power he could wield when necessary. Carefully, without mentioning that it was his customary practise to hide in the toilets whenever games or physical education were timetabled, Thomas explained how he had gone to the cloakroom and had entered the large, white-tiled room just in time to see Timothy crumple to the floor, twitch once or twice and then lie still. He couldn't tell any more since there was no more to tell. He didn't know why Timothy was in the cloakroom nor why he had collapsed and nothing had been said that could give any sort of clue to the affair.

A tear rolled down his almost transparent cheek and the kindly head teacher passed him a tissue and waited while the young lad composed himself. Oh it was so hard for these poor boys; not one of them was without some sort of problem and this boy was no exception. Thomas was albino, evidenced in his pinkish eyes and pale complexion, his eyesight was poor and his dyspraxia meant that his movements were awkward and his hand eye coordination unpredictable. His loving and well-meaning mother, in her ignorance and naivety, had protected and pampered him, overcompensating for his difficulties, and had unintentionally exacerbated his condition by allowing him to become overweight. He had few friends and struggled in mainstream schooling for which reason, and through the interference of his rather more sensible grandmother, he had come here to Sir Randolph's; an environment in which it was hoped he would thrive.

Sir Randolph's was a hospital school for temporarily disabled and more permanently disadvantaged boys. It was run on similar lines to a preparatory school although the age range was wider in order to accommodate a greater number of needy students. Most of the students were boarders and there was a small group who were semipermanent residents at Randolph Manor. Thomas was a member of this small group and was by now so indoctrinated into the institutionalised routine of the school that he no longer pined for home and, truth to tell, was happier here. He loved his mother, as any son should, but he didn't miss her claustrophobic mollycoddling or her overprotective carefulness. Neither did he miss the harsh reality of his grandmother's approach. In fact the only thing he really did miss was his cat. Peanut had been his constant companion since he was three and it had been a wrench to leave his only friend behind. Thus it was that he had been delighted to befriend Timothy, the strange little boy who kept himself to himself. Appearing to be neither happy nor unhappy, quiet and self-contained, Timothy fascinated Thomas. Most of the boys were loud at times and often their stays were brief. A broken leg mended, an illness cured, a long term problem controlled and the boys would say a cheery goodbye at the end of a term or a year. There were a few, like our two protagonists, who needed more constant care but most were either too ill to consider the need for friends or too self-absorbed to even notice that possible friendships were available.

Satisfied with the explanation provided, Fred Barker dismissed the by now more relaxed child, reassuring him that his friend was fine, just resting for a while, and would re-join him later. Thomas muttered his thanks and left, stumbling clumsily on his way to the door and jerking his head back to glance at his superior, expecting the chiding words that did not come. Fred simply smiled in encouragement whilst his mind was remembering another clumsy child who had painstakingly taught himself to control his body's involuntary movements. Dyspraxia was a little understood condition and in his time there had been scarce or no support for the characteristic problems it manifested in sufferers. Fortunately, for Fred the boy, there had been a balanced loving between his parents wherein his mother had provided comfort, organisation and cherishing while his father had taught him physical skills which allowed him to explore the limits of his abilities and to extend his capabilities in as many ways as possible. Thus it was that he found himself here, Head teacher of this unique school, wherein he tried to help others find themselves in a similar way to that in which he had also been helped.

He smiled to himself and nodded wisely in the knowledge that this child could and would turn out to be something special and that he, Fred, was there to guide and support him through his adolescence. He was pleased that Thomas had found a kindred spirit in Timothy.

Timothy; now there was an enigma. The beautiful, self-contained and independent child seemed so alone and yet he was content and appeared to want for nothing more than the bare minimum of parenting and nurture. He was intelligent and able, almost to the point of being gifted and talented, and he learned quickly and easily; passing exams with little apparent effort. But there was something about the child, something more than the mild epilepsy from which he suffered, that drew others to him and aroused curiosity in many, both old and young. He was often to be found talking to matron or cook in preference to playing out on the field with the other students or, more frequently, he would take himself off to some secluded spot where he revelled in his self-imposed isolation. It was this penchant for aloneness that had enabled his condition to go undiagnosed for so long.

$$***$$

At first, Rosa was in denial. She had been determined that her son should go to the local school and mix with ordinary children from the village. Despite Simon's insistence that his obviously intelligent son deserved the best education money could buy, she had ignored his wishes and enrolled him at St John's JMI School. To begin with, Timothy settled in to the daily routine, although he never really formed any close friendships. However, six months on and half way through the spring term, Rosa received a summons to the head teacher's office. Teaching staff were concerned about his occasionally odd behaviour.

"Nothing naughty you must understand, Mrs Cooper," the middle-aged master assured, "it's just that he appears to lose concentration at times. He seems to sort of... switch off for a few seconds. Have you noticed this at all?" She had not.

And so it was that after long discussions with Simon and Eleanor, which resulted in them all agreeing that an investigation should be instigated, and after several visits to Harley Street and an associated Great Ormond Street clinic, Timothy was diagnosed with mild epilepsy. Throughout the whole process, Timothy had remained calm and completely unchanged by the disruption to his normal pattern. Indeed he appeared to be entirely ignorant of his 'absences' although he would occasionally seem to be a little disorientated afterwards. Nevertheless it was decided that he should transfer to Sir Randolph's where he could be observed and monitored in an environment designed to cater for these and other such idiosyncrasies. Rosa, having conceded to this temporary arrangement, desperately hoped that he could and would one day return to her original plan.

***

"So what do you want to do then?" Thomas spoke first, not really expecting an answer. A long silence followed, during which neither boy moved; a silence which was suddenly pierced by the shrill ring of a telephone. The lads jumped in unison, startled eyes wide, as they realised their folly and then laughed together in embarrassment. The spell was broken and soon the two were plotting and planning how they would use their unaccustomed freedom whilst they had the whole school to themselves, or so it seemed.

Chapter Twelve

Pearly white iridescence, perfectly formed, exquisitely perfumed and nestled at its heart, a solitary diamond dewdrop...

The delicate perfume invaded his olfactory senses and demanded that he open his eyes to see from whence this pleasant aroma emanated. Resting proudly against the crystal side of a single stem vase, head slightly bowed with the heaviness of its petals, a white rose, perfection in its form, fluttered gently in the light breeze from an open window and shared its beauty with all who would see and smell.

An involuntary smile crossed Tomo's face before it turned to a grimace as he tried to pull himself up to rest against the pillows. His groan brought Nurse Isabella to his bedside, soothing him and pressing him back down to a totally prostrate position. "Wait," she commanded, "Doctor Baird would like to speak to you before you move too much." Alarm bells rang in Tomo's head. How much longer must he lie here? How long had he already lain here? Realising he had absolutely no idea what day it was, let alone what week, month or hour, he allowed himself to be ordered and did as he was told. The kindly nurse disappeared and since he felt a little more alert than he had for a long time, Tomo turned his head to more closely inspect his surroundings. He was in a private room which was obviously part of a well-equipped hospital with the usual monitors and gadgets attached to the walls and bedside trolleys. There was the ubiquitous saline drip attached to his arm, the bleeping heart monitor and most irritatingly of all, the blanket covered cage over his legs which obliterated his view of the window opposite. To his right was the door and to his left was an array of cupboards and shelves in front of which was an armchair strategically placed for the use of visitors. Visitors? Had he had any? Did anyone even know he was here? Come to think of it, did he even know where he was? He grunted with wry amusement at the ridiculousness of his situation and determined to ask that helpful nurse to do some explaining.

***

Two months! Surely not that long? For as long as he could, Tomo tried to not think about the dreadful thing he had been told; the thing that he had known all along but had chosen to ignore in the belief that if he didn't acknowledge it then it couldn't be true. 'Severed above the knee'; it sounded so clinical and ordinary when you said it like that. But the reality? This would change his whole life; everything. But no! He must not think about that, he is a soldier, this is just a little obstacle, he will sleep again and when he wakes everything will be just as it was before. His leg will mend and he'll soon be back at the front line with his mates. Even the mud, cold, noise and horror of it all would be better than this bland, emptiness.

***

The days passed with mundane monotony. Each morning he was greeted with a cheery, "Good morning soldier!" and a lukewarm cup of tea which was always too sweet. Why had no one bothered to ask whether he liked sugar in his tea? Why had he not bothered to mention it? Truth to tell it seemed so unimportant that he dismissed the complaint before he had made it. Nurse Isabella was kindness itself in a distant sort of way and Tomo realised that he had come to rely on her omnipresence and even looked forward to her maternal fussing and chiding. He knew nothing about her other than that she was a nurse, she was middle aged, maybe forty something, plain although not unattractive, and the kindest person he'd ever met. Nothing was too much trouble and she bore his bad tempered grumbles with a smile and a soothing word or two. She provided him with clean pyjamas, toiletries, towels and a daily newspaper which he never read. There was a growing pile of them in the little cupboard next to his bed; perhaps he would look at them tomorrow… She brought him regular meals and never complained when he ate so little and wasted so much. And there was always a little treat such as some fruit or a chocolate bar to tempt him to eat something rather than nothing. One day she even brought him a bottle of wine. Surprised, he

59

asked her why to which she replied, "It's my birthday. I thought you might like to join me in a glass or two?" He nodded in assent and she produced two plastic cups from her capacious apron pocket and proceeded to pour a little wine into each. Expertly she heaved him up the bed and plumped the pillows behind his head. The cage no longer encased his legs beneath the blankets and he studiously avoided looking at the empty space where his left leg should have lain. Still he avoided the subject of his missing appendage and despite the many doctors who attended him on a regular basis he hadn't voiced the concerns and potential future issues that, although never far from his thoughts, he constantly repressed. "Healing nicely!" was the repeated diagnosis and, "soon be up and about," was the general prognosis.

More often than not Tomo truly believed that he would be better off dead.

Nevertheless, today was Isabella's birthday and he should make the effort to at least acknowledge her goodness to him. Accordingly he lifted his glass and raised a weak smile, "Many happy returns," he bade her as he sipped the ruby red wine.

Perhaps it was the combination of wine and the many drugs he seemed to be filled with, but before long he began to feel more relaxed and light hearted than he had for a very long time. His tongue loosened and without really intending to, he found himself pouring out all the pent up frustrations and suppressed emotions that had locked him in his self-imposed psychological isolation.

First came the tears. Involuntarily they coursed down his cheeks in silent rivulets and he made no attempt to brush them aside but cried unashamedly. Self-pity, delayed shock, overwhelming despair and panic at the thought of what next all combined to drown him in suicidal depression. But this emotional reaction did not last and soon the tears became those of frustration and anger. Anger at his weakness, anger at his situation, anger at his overbearing and often absent father, anger at his weak and self-absorbed mother, at his 'oh so clever' brother, at the medics, the doctors and even at Nurse

Isabella who sat silently at his bedside, stroking his hand and nodding wisely as his outpouring of grief washed through him and carried out its necessary catharsis.

At last he was drained of all emotion and all energy. Isabella gently lowered the pillows and advised him to try to sleep, advice which he didn't hesitate to follow except to take her hand and briefly touch it to his lips whispering, "Thank you." She smiled and her blue eyes drilled into his. "You'll be alright." she reassured him.

As she began to leave the room, his eyes flew open again and he called to her in a far stronger and more imperious voice than he had previously mustered, "Oh and thank you for the flower."

"The flower?" she looked surprised as she glanced in the direction he was indicating, "Oh, how lovely," she smiled, she paused thoughtfully for a moment and then, "but it wasn't me that put it there," and she was gone.

If she had not put it there, then who had? He was not aware of having had any visitors. Indeed he had made it quite clear that he didn't want to see anyone and even resented the intrusion of the medical staff at times. Of course he could appreciate the necessity of nurses and doctors and he certainly couldn't do much for himself. Oh they wheeled him to the bathroom in a rickety old chair and he managed to clean his own teeth and feed himself now but he refused point blank to take a bath or shower. There was no way he was going to look at it; that would make it far too real. This way he could go on believing that everything would go back to how it was before. But mostly he still just wished that he had died in that explosion...

Chapter Thirteen

Blissfully happy, the two young boys played in the mud by the edge of the lake. Oblivious to the rain and the chill air, they dug channels, trenches, dams and bridges. A whole empire spread out before them and they were the wise rulers of their kingdom. Frogs watched them with bulging eyes and throbbing throats and ducks and moorhens piped and quacked in chorus with the incessant dripping of rain from leaves to surface. Neither boy spoke but their communication was evident as they worked as one to stop the rain from washing away their creation.

***

"Trouble, with a capital T!" that's what he said they were in. Mr Stamp, the site manager, had found them and dragged them back, dumping them unceremoniously in the communal shower room and demanding they wait there while he, "Fetches 'elp!" They looked at each other, trying to compose their faces and feeling that they ought to be trembling with fear at the prospect of facing their punishment. However, neither of them felt afraid and uncontrollable laughter threatened to bubble up at the most inappropriate of moments. Thomas thought he was the happiest he had ever been but how could that be so when he was about to get thoroughly told off for enjoying his afternoon? It made no sense and so he didn't try to make sense of it; even if it meant he had to pay the price later, it was certainly worth it.

Two muddy, bedraggled boys confronted his gaze when Fred Barker entered the shower room. Struggling to compose his face which was trying to insist he smile at them, he spoke gruffly, "Get yourselves cleaned up and warmly dressed and then come to my room." He tried to sound stern but the twinkle in his eye was not missed by Timothy who winked at Thomas, mouthing, "It's going to be ok." as he poked out a cheeky tongue at his head teacher's retreating back. This was a different side of Timothy, unseen before; his newly found confidence coming to the fore enabled him to be braver than he actually felt. Still, it wouldn't be the first time he had been chided for forgetting the time, the elements and any instructions he had received, and it almost certainly would not be the last!

A short while later, two rosy cheeked, damp haired and squeaky clean boys knocked tentatively on Fred Barker's door.

"Come in," responded an imperious voice.

At first they couldn't see Mr Barker who was not sitting in his usual position behind the heavy oak desk, but stepping further through the doorway, they saw him standing on the other side of the room with his back to the old-fashioned grate in which glowed and crackled a roaring fire. Placed near the fire were three armchairs and a coffee table upon which rested three steaming mugs of cocoa, a plate of crumpets, knives, butter and jam.

Without preamble, Fred passed each boy a toasting fork and showed them how to place a crumpet securely on the prongs and hold it close to the flames, not too close, to toast it to perfection. Soon all three were munching contentedly on hot buttered crumpets spread with lashings of jam, as though they hadn't a care in the world.

Nevertheless, there was tension in spite of the camaraderie and it was Thomas who, in his innocence, first broached the subject of their misdemeanours. "Excuse me Mr Barker, but aren't you going to be cross with us?"

"Well now, let me see..." Fred put his finger across his lips and furrowed his brow in concentrated thought, "What do you think I should do about it?" he asked. There was a long pause during which no one chewed, sipped or spoke and then, "I think the onus is on us to apologise and to enquire as to what we can do to make amends." The sombre look on Timothy's face and the genuine air of contrition, combined with the maturity of expression in his words, told of other similar situations and the skill of an experienced actor in his attempt to placate his elder. Fred could contain himself no longer and a huge rumble of laughter rolled up from his belly and emanated from his mouth while the two boys looked on in astonishment. When the merriment finally subsided the older man drew the two boys to him in a swift avuncular hug and pressed them back into their seats saying, "I expect you'll find it hard to believe, but I was a boy like you two once. There's nothing wrong with a bit of mud from time to time, just don't make too much of a habit of it or I'll have matron complaining about the cost of soap powder again! Now let me see, where did I put that letter?"

***

And so it was that just thirty minutes later, the two boys found themselves packing their bags and chattering excitedly, planning adventures for the next three weeks to come. Going home! Timothy could hardly believe it. He had been told in no uncertain terms that he was to stay at the school until Christmas; such a long way off! He had swallowed his tears and tried so hard to understand that it was 'for his own good.' However, here he was, not only going home but taking Thomas with him. Thomas; well that was a mixed blessing really. On the one hand it would be nice to have someone to play with and Thomas was good at joining in with whatever he suggested. Yet on the other hand, Timothy, even at his tender age, knew that he needed time and space to himself. What would Thomas do when he isolated himself in his customary way?

Timothy's excitement was subdued, in keeping with his usually reserved reaction to sudden changes. He was curious. Why this sudden alteration? And why was Thomas with him? Nevertheless his heart swelled when he was met by a beaming Carrie who smothered him in a hug and kissed him sloppily on the cheek before embracing Thomas, who was nearly as big as she was, in an equally enthusiastic hug. Thomas was taken aback; his undemonstrative, although similarly suffocating, mother had rarely hugged him and yet this total stranger was welcoming him as a long lost friend and he was at a loss as to how to respond. However, he needn't have been concerned for Eleanor quickly came to his rescue and dispatched the excited Carrie to fetch refreshment for them all before sending them up to bed. It was late, past midnight, and the rest of the household were already sleeping. "Off you go. There'll be time for explanations tomorrow. Now you need to sleep and so do I." The boys were swiftly dispatched to their room as Carrie fussed around them and made sure they had fresh pyjamas and towels, "an' make sure you clean your teef," she insisted.

As it happened, Timothy needn't have worried at all. Much to his amazement there, curled fluffily in a glossy heap in the middle of the spare bed, which was to be Thomas' for the next few weeks, utterly inexplicably, was Peanut. The tortoiseshell cat purred contentedly whilst totally ignoring the repeated nudgings of Snowball who seemed determined, even at this late hour, to make him play. Thomas scooped up his beloved cat and buried his face in the warm fur. Instantly Timothy realised that Thomas would be perfectly content to spend time with his pet while he was occupied with his own, so very important and individual business. Carrie shooed the little dog away before tucking the two boys into their beds and turning off the light. "Nigh nigh, sleep tigh'" she said softly, "See oo in a mornin'." Before long all was silent apart from the gentle breathing, rhythmic purring and night time creakings of the old house.

**

He was her delight, this golden child who filled her with such joy and hope despite her aging bones and failing senses. No blood relation but the son of her adopted niece-come-daughter's widowed husband, she embraced him with unquestioning wholehearted acceptance as her grandson; no questions asked. Eleanor gazed out of the window, watching the two small boys engrossed in their play. Round their ankles ran Snowball. Alternately yapping excitedly and jumping up and biting their sleeves in mock attack, he joined in their play whilst ensuring that he knew where they were and could guard and watch them as they strayed further and further from the house.

The long lawn swept down toward the stream that ran through the paddock beyond the garden wall. Ten tall willow trees waved their branches, bending with the wind and sweeping the ground with their long green fingers as the warm wind stirred their slumber. 'It was the willow trees that gave the old house its name; Willow Lodge' Eleanor reflected, as she packed away her untouched embroidery and made her way to the kitchen.

Elsa was making lunch, watched fixedly by Peanut who waited ready to pounce on any small morsel of cold meat that might accidently fall to the floor.

"Snowball has gone with them." Elsa spoke without turning around.

"Yes, I saw them," replied Eleanor. The two women worked together in companionable silence for a few minutes until the simple meal was prepared and ready to be served when the hungry mouths returned.

Since her visit to Old Bess Elsa had watched. She had watched and understood, accepted but not interfered, just as Old Bess had advised. She had been troubled when the early diagnosis of epilepsy, or petit mal, had been made, since she knew that neither Rosa nor Simon would understand the real reason behind his apparent malady. Neither could she explain it to them in anything other than a medical sense; one by which drugs and treatments might try to make him better but one whereby he would not be changed.

She had been alarmed when the family made the decision to send him away to Sir Randolph's for she would not be able to watch over him so closely. Consequently, the news that he was coming home was greeted with quiet satisfaction and great relief. For a time, at least, she could continue to guide and watch this precious child.

Elsa patted her apron pocket, reassuring herself that it was still there and reminding herself to place it on his pillow for him to find tonight.

Chapter Fourteen

Sunlight streaming through the frosted window lit up all the specks of airborne dust and gave them an undeserved richness of gold and silver. Their glory danced over Sally's closed eyelids and prized them open in their demand that she awake and enjoy the day. Luxuriously she stretched, anticipating a hearty breakfast and hot mug of tea before making her way across the yard to tend the cattle. Slipping her feet into her cosy slippers and pulling her fleecy dressing gown around her slight form, she made her way down the narrow stairway. Instead of the warm glow and appetising smell she had expected, she was met by an empty room and a hungry cat. Where were Dora and Daniel? To begin with she was unfazed although puzzled, and simply lifted the kettle onto the hob and began to prepare some food. Everything was where it should be and the freshly baked bread was ready sliced for toasting, the milk in a jug and the pan of porridge waiting to be heated. But there was no sign of the perpetrator of these preparations. Perhaps there had been some sort of minor emergency in the yard, thought Sally as she hurriedly fed herself.

A short while later she crossed the yard to the big barn expecting to begin the morning chores, only to discover that all had been done. Still puzzling over this strangeness, she made her way back to the farmhouse. She had not previously considered Dora and Daniel's presence in her home. She had been numbed by the traumatic experience of hospital and unaccustomed sickness and had simply accepted everything that had happened since that fateful day. But now she began to question. Who were they? Where had they come from? How did they know about her situation?

"Don't worry about it." The unexpected voice startled her out of her reverie.

"Wha... what did you say?" she turned swiftly and there standing close by the big old Aga was a small golden haired boy. In his hand was a plastic farm cow and by his feet a toy tractor and plough.

"You really don't need to worry," he repeated in a surprisingly adult tone for one who seemed so young. "They came while you needed them but now you are fine and they are needed somewhere else. I don't know where..." his youth became evident in the dropping of his tone and his uncertainty and yet it lasted only briefly and he continued more strongly, "But you'll be alright now and anyway you aren't going to be alone for very much longer."

Shocked and surprised, an overwhelming sense of isolation swept through her and she recognised the despairing depth of her longing for partnership that he was holding before her. She almost felt guilty for wanting even so very little. Why could she not be content to remain alone?

"Everyone needs someone." He read her thoughts and responded, "It's perfectly natural you know and you shouldn't be ashamed of possessing a basic need." Unbidden tears flowed silently down her cheeks and she instinctively held out her hand to the boy. And yet as she took his hand in hers and began to pull him toward her, his body gradually faded and became insubstantial. She closed her eyes in an exaggerated blink and when she opened them again he was gone. In her hand was a stem, upon the head of which was, perfectly poised, a single white rose.

***

Elsa was relieved that it was she who found him first. Thomas had been almost incoherent in his anxiety to explain. Elsa calmed him gently and pressed him into the old rocking chair, soothing him with her words, "Take your time and tell me carefully."

"He's in the mud," was all Thomas could mutter while his teeth chattered, not with chill, but with the rush of cold adrenalin that wetted his brow and brought tears to his eyes.

"Show me." Elsa pulled him to his feet and wrapped him in her cardigan despite the warm late-afternoon sun. He led her across the sloping lawn towards a favourite playing spot near the edge of the stream where it broadened out into a small pond or lake.

Before they reached him, Elsa could see him lying spread-eagled on the ground, face down in the mud. Beside him was Snowball, yapping excitedly and licking Timothy's dirty face. In his hands were tightly grasped a plastic cow and a small green tractor.

***

On this occasion, Elsa chose to not disclose the afternoon's occurrences to Timothy's parents. Rosa and Simon were busy; each pursuing their hectic business and social commitments as was often the case during weekdays. Weekends were set aside for family and without fail, time would be spent with Timothy and now with Thomas too. Eleanor of course, knew immediately that something had happened and Elsa did not hide her knowledge from this woman who had become her closest friend and confidante. Once the two boys were safely ensconced in front of the TV watching some crazy adventure, Eleanor drew her aside and quizzed her closely. There was no doubt of their mutual concern for the child, nor was there any reason to suppose that the medication had not been administered correctly by little Carrie who had undertaken to be responsible for the delivering the small pink pills to her little brother. No, there was something more to this. Both women knew it but neither felt confident enough to voice their intuitive knowledge. They would watch and wait, time would tell if all was tumbling upside down.

***

69

Long after the boys should have been asleep, Elsa tiptoed into their room. She bent low over Thomas' sleeping form and shooed a complaining cat from under his covers. Then she crossed to Timothy and as she leaned over to place the mended soldier on his bedside table, was surprised to see him staring intently at her, his bright blue eyes boring into hers as he muttered, "Everyone needs someone..." His eyes closed and his muscles relaxed and as they did so a plastic cow fell to the floor where it came to rest against the rear wheel of a green toy tractor.

***

The coughing and spluttering of the old green Ferguson tractor woke Sally from the deep slumber into which she had fallen. Prising her eyelids open and forcing her stiffened limbs into action, she struggled up from the sofa and crossed the kitchen to peer through the window and into the lane. Slowly her eyes focused on the scene wherein her cows were meandering in their usual bovine solemnity toward the yard and milking parlour. Following them was the tractor responsible for her rude awakening. Her first thought was to glance at the ancient cuckoo clock that ticked its tock above the mantelpiece. Five pm! Right on time. Of course the cows always knew when it was time but who was this that had released them from the meadow and was driving them toward their twice daily relief?

Hastily, she pulled on the comfortable wellingtons and donned her mackintosh before heading out to cross the yard and greet this welcome newcomer. It was, however, some time before she could actually speak to him since the noise of the tractor and the lowing of the cows precluded all conversation. And so it was that they worked in harmony to install the cows in the parlour and begin the process of milking the small herd. Not until the last cow was emptied, washed down and released into the holding pen and the machinery shut down, were they able to converse. Even before Sally could begin to ask, Tom introduced himself saying, "Thank you so much for giving me this opportunity. I got here as soon as I could. I know I can do the job and I won't let you down. The cottage is perfect, just a lick of paint or two and a bit of a scrub down and it will be wonderfully warm and cosy." What on earth was he talking about? She hadn't given anyone any opportunity... had she? Never one to waste words she responded gruffly, "You'd better come and see the rest of the farm and then I'll make you a cuppa. I think you have some explaining to do!"

A short while later he stepped through the old door into the warmth of the kitchen, sliding his boots off in the lobby and hanging his battered hat on an appropriate hook. His gaze slid round the room and took in its homely neatness and cosy comfort until, with a shock of recognition, he saw, resting in a silver single stem vase, the very same rose, or so it seemed, that he had last seen on that dismal day not so very long ago.

Chapter Fifteen

The funeral had been awful. The weather, never kind in this part of the world, did its best to cry enough tears for everyone. 'Everyone' amounted to a handful of villagers and fishermen, a few friends and neighbours, himself and Sandra who alternately sobbed into her already sodden handkerchief and shot sidelong glances at him to see if he had noticed how distressed she was. He wasn't at all sure that she was distressed in the slightest. Her behaviour, since the dreadful news had sunk in, had been extraordinary and he couldn't understand her at all, perhaps because she couldn't understand or explain herself. There was no doubt that she was profoundly affected by this double calamity and it appeared that he was the only relative on whom she could rely and on whom she could pour her toxic mix of grief and outrage.

To say that she was not coping would be a major understatement. At times she seemed balanced and almost happy to play lady of the house and at others she was simply like a lost child. In between times she varied between being argumentative, determined and stubborn and in flirting sickeningly with him. Of course it had not been long yet and he tried to be as sympathetic toward her as she would allow whilst also attempting to control his own emotional upheavals. Aunt Aggie and Uncle Joe had been his only surviving relatives, apart from Sandra for whom he did not wish to become responsible in any sense. He would have to make arrangements for her care and what was to become of him? His ambition to study, to make something of himself, seemed doomed to be discarded. First it was lack of money and now it was both that and this unexpected responsibility for his cousin and for winding up her parents' affairs. It was no use expecting her to be able to negotiate her way through the probate process. Neither could she continue to live in the cottage by herself, nor was there any way that he was going to stay there with her! Besides he could not carry on his uncle's fishing business by himself.

He closed his eyes, trying to pray sincerely for his aunt and uncle but the words would not come and irreverent thoughts crowded his mind. Neither of them had been regular church goers and he could not ignore the hypocrisy of this expectation of a show of false faith wherein it is all in the mouth and not in the heart. Nevertheless, he kept his head bowed throughout the short service and dutifully shook the hands of those who came to offer sympathy and consolation; thanking them and inviting them to join him and Sandra in the village hall for tea and cake, the best they could offer in place of a wake.

It was as he was about to leave the little chapel that he saw the small boy with the white rose and it was as he crossed the memorial gardens to the village hall that he noticed the tall, austere woman talking to Sandra. He stopped in surprise. Sandra was smiling a full, genuine smile which lit up her face and made her seem much younger and more beautiful. He could not hear what they were saying but he saw her nod her head in agreement and lightly hug the older woman before continuing on her way to the wake whilst the other walked briskly away before disappearing behind a large yew tree.

It was with a shock of recognition that Sandra had seen the lady from the bus as she crossed the gardens from the chapel. Bethany stepped onto the path a little way ahead of her and held out her hand whilst smiling broadly. It was almost as though she had been enveloped in an all-encompassing mist of emotion that had obscured even who she was and this woman, just as she had mysteriously cured both the hangover and the snipped fringe, equally inexplicably wiped away the mist. Bethany did not speak; she simply touched Sandra's forehead and all the angst, pain, confusion and anger that had wracked her heart for so long, seemed to fade away. Sandra found herself smiling broadly as a feeling of contentment and peacefulness washed over her.

"Come and see me soon?" Bethany whispered and pushed a slip of paper into Sandra's hand. She nodded in affirmation and briefly hugged the older woman before continuing on her way, smiling the first genuine smile to have lighted her face for a long time.

***

The small boy pushed his hand into hers as they walked briskly across the gardens. She smiled down at his glowing face with its halo of golden hair as he turned his upward to hers. Words were not necessary as she guided him across the tussocks of lush grass which punctuated the, by now, green fields. Soon, it seemed, they glided over some invisible landscape as their feet were lost in the rising dewy mist. They walked on clouds in a timeless void, each knowing the other and in total harmony. Was that a humble cottage they passed by? The sole occupant waving to them as her apron billowed in the sudden breeze? A seagull cried its raucous call, and they were gone.

***

There followed a significant change in Sandra's behaviour. She became somehow more humble, more considerate and at the same time more distant from him. Tom was able to relax and drop the constant guard with which he had protected himself from her wild mood swings. Thus it was that when the lawyer came to explain the contents of her parent's wills, she presented herself as a semi-mature, confident young woman. It was no surprise to discover that there was little money and that the cottage would have to be sold to meet inheritance tax and other expenses. However, there was a trust fund for Sandra and she would receive a monthly sum great enough to provide for her needs until she was twenty-one, at which time she would inherit any remaining monies. It would at least ensure that she had an adequate start in her adult, and hopefully qualified, life. As for Tom, there was provision made for him to receive the proceeds from the sale of Joe's fishing business. It was a nice gesture but in reality would realise only a small sum since the equipment was old-fashioned, the location poor and the business, such as it was, failing. Nevertheless, Tom was grateful for small mercies and it would certainly be enough to set him on his feet, mend his bike and begin his journey away from this place.

***

"Timothy! I'm talking to you," Elsa repeated and gently shook his shoulder. He slumped slowly and awkwardly towards her and she caught him before he crashed to the floor. She saw the glazed look in his eyes which confirmed his condition and carefully lifted him from the stool on which he perched precariously. She laid him on the old ottoman trunk and covered him with a fleecy rug before settling beside him to watch until he recovered.

A short while later, a grin slowly spread across his face and his bright blue eyes flickered open and closed once or twice before he murmured, "Thank you Bethany, they'll be alright now won't they?"

"Hush child, of course they will," Elsa whispered as he stretched luxuriously and curling into the foetal position, fell sound asleep.

Elsa rose quietly, pulled the rug more closely round her sleeping charge and knowing that he was safe now, tiptoed out of the room. She was surprised to find Thomas crouched outside the door and looking tearful and frightened. He was almost incoherent in his response to her questioning and so she ushered him through to the kitchen and prepared him some hot chocolate to drink. The pale boy had an ethereal quality in spite of his size and the hot beverage passing from the mug to his lips was in stark contrast to the whiteness of his skin. Soothed and calmer he began to explain how he and Timothy had been playing at the table when Snowball had twice barked sharply causing Peanut to jump in alarm and run away. Thomas had run after him as fast as his chubby and unfit legs could manage. But Peanut had disappeared. Add to that the fact that Thomas knew what Snowball's bark indicated, and here the tears began to well from his eyes again, and that he had not done as he should to help Timothy to stay safe, and Thomas's anguish can be understood. Elsa held the troubled boy in her arms until his shuddering and sniffing ceased and she could reassure him that all would be well. She took him upstairs to freshen him up and change his clothes and smiled to herself at the delighted expression on his face when he saw there, curled on his pillow, Peanut; bedraggled, muddy, and proudly offended but quite prepared to forgive Snowball, provided he gave due warning of his intended explosive barking next time he felt it necessary to perform the act.

Quietly musing to herself later that evening, Elsa realised the importance of what Thomas had told her. Snowball could sense when Timothy was going to have a 'turn'! Of course, hadn't Old Bess implied something of the sort…?

Chapter Sixteen

The prosthetic limb hurt him. It rubbed and chaffed the soft scar tissue of his stump, that horrible word for his horrible wound, he could hardly bear to think the word, let alone pronounce it. It had taken hours of patience from Nurse Isabella to persuade him to even look at his leg. Even now he avoided it at every possible opportunity, refusing to apply the creams and lotions that might toughen up his skin and help him to heal.

He could never heal. This wound went too deep. He was angry, so overwhelmingly angry at the people and politicians whose crass judgements had, in his eyes, been totally responsible for his plight, that he had lost all reason as far as doing the best for himself was concerned. He refused to see anyone other than the doctors, Nurse Isabella and the lawyer who was seeking compensation on his behalf. Many times his mother had been turned away by an apologetic receptionist and even his father had not been able to demand entrance to the room. Tomo was wallowing in his own misery and something needed to be done...

***

Thomas had left a few days before. Apparently his mother was well enough to have him home for the last week of the summer before the autumn term began. Timothy missed him. Truth to tell, despite his former foreboding, he had very much enjoyed having Thomas at his side. The two boys shared an appreciation of silent play and although there were times when they had laughed uproariously together, there had been many more when the intensity of their quiet play had combined their spirits in an intuitive understanding of each other. Timothy listlessly picked at the loose threads on the bottom edge of his counterpane. He was sitting on the floor close to the bed, contemplating his return to St Randolph's. It wasn't so much that he didn't want to go back there, it was just that here he felt closer to

77

everything; nature, loved ones, Snowball and those invisible presences that were ever present. He closed his eyes and leaned back against the soft bedding that hung from the edge of his bed.

***

The first thing he noticed was the exquisite perfume that emanated from somewhere on his right. Gradually the smell became overlain by something more pungent and clinical and he opened his eyes a little in order to observe his surroundings. The room was stark in its plainness. White walls with no pictures, one window with a simple blind and no drapes, a pale green painted wardrobe and chest of drawers placed on one wall and an ordinary chair and desk on which was placed a single lamp and a glass of water; in the glass stood a single white rose.

Finally, his gaze came to rest on the iron bedstead. Gradually his eyes worked from the foot to the head where he was surprised to see a sad pair of deep brown eyes gazing directly at him. The look of astonishment on the face of the owner of the eyes was matched by the suddenness with which Timothy sat up and smiled broadly at Tomo.

"J?" whispered Tomo, hardly daring to breathe let alone believe what he was seeing.

"Yeah bro, it's me." There was none of the usual exuberance in J's voice as he continued wistfully, "You did better than me this time." For some time Tomo said nothing; his mouth worked but his tongue would not form the words and his eyes would not leave J's face.

"Wh… what d… do you mean?" he finally managed to stutter.

"Well look at you man!" came the quick retort, "You're alive, you can think and pretty soon you will walk again. And as for me, well I bought it mate. I never even made it to the front line, not even out of the country. Damned bomb! I nearly had it disarmed too but hey, it must have had my number! So stop feeling sorry for yourself now; get out there bro and live."

Before he could stop himself the words were out, "But what have I got to live for?"

Boiling rage seethed in Tomo; all the pent up anger and jealousy that had plagued his childhood. All the disappointment he had caused his father by not being like his brother and all the times his father had failed to notice how hard he had tried to do and be as he wanted. He reached out his hand, grabbed the glass containing the rose and flung it hard against the far wall. It shattered with a resounding crash as splinters of glass flew everywhere. The rose flew in an arc straight towards Jackie who instinctively threw his arms across his face to protect himself from the missile.

Once silence had resettled in the room, and without removing his arm from his face, Jackie began to speak; "I always wanted to be like you. You were clever, strong and had such courage. I could never be like you and so I acted the fool, the clown, the entertainer. And just as I made people laugh and feel good about themselves, so they failed to notice that I wasn't as clever or as successful as they thought. I became the master of misdirection, hoodwinking my way through life. Nevertheless, deep down inside I knew I was playing a dangerous game and one day it would all come to a sticky end. Little did I know just how sticky or how soon it would be. I'm sorry for the times you were ignored or unfairly chastised because of me. I never wanted you to suffer, believe me, I really did want to be like you but I just couldn't do it."

Tomo slipped awkwardly and painfully from the bed and sat on the floor facing the half turned and face-covered form in the corner of the room as it sighed deeply before continuing, "Dad was hard on you because he knew you were better than me. He knew you could succeed at anything you put your mind to but he also knew that you were jealous of me and he was afraid that you would attempt to be like me. He knew how false my act was. He never spoke of it but I know he knew." There was a pause and then the figure turned back and moved his arm from over his face. Tomo was startled to find himself staring into the piercing blue eyes framed by curly blonde hair of the small boy he had first seen, so long ago it seemed, in the field hospital. How could he be here and who on earth is he?

"He's hurting." The boy spoke softly in a tone that was somehow both his and J's, "He needs you. Learn to walk, go to him before it's too late. He will not be here for much longer and there is reconciliation to be done before his time comes." Timothy shuffled slowly forward and proffering the rose with one hand, slipped the other over the larger one that rested on the floor nearby. Carefully he lifted the hand and placed it gently on the folded pyjama leg that covered Tomo's stump. Gradually, using Tomo's fingers under his own, he explored the creases and bumps of the scar, feeling its shape and texture and familiarising him with himself so that he could learn to love who and what he had become. Tomo closed his eyes as Timothy's caress seemed to drain all anger, hurt and pain from both his body and his soul. He turned his hand under Timothy's small one, grasped it and raised it to his lips...

***

He was surprised to find himself on the floor when he awoke. Nurse Isabella was sitting beside him and holding his hand in hers while she gently patted the back of it to rouse him. At first he thought it had all been a dream but as he allowed Nurse Isabella to raise him to his bed, he saw the shards of glass still where they had fallen. On his pillow lay the single white rose.

As Nurse Isabella quietly prepared to leave the room, he called to her, "Nurse! Please pass me the jar of skin cream. I think I'll rub some onto my stump now..." She smiled to herself as she turned to give him the pot of cream. Her work here was done. She hugged him briefly and was gone...

Chapter Seventeen

It had been a punishing game. Evenly matched teams fought hard despite the pouring rain and sodden pitch. The goalkeeper, looking like a mud wrestler rather than a rugby player, was almost blinded by the dripping wetness and earthy mire that plastered his hair to his forehead and streamed constantly down his face. Perhaps it was this that contributed to the disaster and there is no doubt that the weather played its part too.

At eleven years old, Timothy had found a passion for sport. Although somewhat surprised, Simon encouraged his previously rather isolated son and as a spectator, supported his son whenever possible. Swimming and Tennis were for the warmer months and Rugby in the winter. At first there had been concerns about his epileptic episodes and the possibility of putting himself in unnecessary danger, but the doctors assured Rosa that he was as safe on the playing field as he would be in his own back garden and that there were plenty of people to watch him and protect if necessary. His medication was effective and Timothy was adamant that he would not be stopped by his 'label'. He argued vehemently that if he was fit enough to go to ordinary school, as his mother had decreed, then he was fit enough to partake of normal schoolboy activities. A developing stubbornness had made him difficult to appease and, thus it was, that Simon and Thomas watched from the sidelines on that miserable Saturday afternoon.

Now fourteen, Timothy's favoured position was 'flanker'. His diminutive size meant he could slip in-between the larger players and he was fast; running like the wind whenever the lozenge shaped missile came flying his way. Time after time he scooped up the ball as it came out of a ruck and time after time he weaved through the opposing players in his mad dash for the line. Thomas roared with delight as he trudged up and down through the mud, watching his friend. Often Timothy was successful; and on the occasions the ball was wrestled from him, he simply shrugged and renewed his efforts. Nothing he did was ever done half-heartedly.

As with the experiences of most very young children, Timothy did not question. Mercifully, his epileptic spells were not remembered by him and he was rarely surprised to find himself tucked up in some safe spot that he didn't remember finding for himself. Nevertheless, he knew that there was something odd about his experiences, not dreams but real occurrences, which remained vivid in his mind. He could not explain to himself, let alone to anyone else, how these things happened, and so he simply did not try. He accepted that they were a part of him and he flowed with life as he overflowed with enthusiasm, especially for sport, nature and his music.

It wasn't until he was thirteen and was deemed fit enough to rejoin mainstream schooling that he began to realise that his experiences were not the norm for others. His condition was controlled by drugs which did not interfere with his everyday life and much like any young teenager he threw himself into sport, music, Scouting and outdoor activities alongside his education. His only sadness at this time was in leaving Thomas at St Randolph's. Latterly he had begun to understand that Thomas would never be able to lead as full and active a life as exciting as his own and it was with regret that they parted ways. Nevertheless, Thomas often came to visit and was always welcomed as part of the already higgledy-piggledy family.

The streaming rain seemed determined to blind even the most keen-sighted and Timothy brushed the wet hair from his face in an attempt to see more clearly. The ball was there, right in front of him but veering off to the left as it bounced on the ground, its elliptical shape dictating the unpredictability of its ultimate direction. Timothy literally threw himself at the object, at exactly the same moment as 'Big Boy', the aptly nicknamed prop, Bob, launched his whole weight after the prize. The resulting clash of heads and bodies resounded around the stadium, followed by a stunned silence whilst the players and spectators alike were briefly frozen to the spot in horror. After a few more seemingly endless moments, a sigh of relief indicated that at least one of the casualties was alive and conscious. Big Boy heaved himself to his feet and rubbing his head, which already sported a sizeable 'egg', glanced perfunctorily at the prone body he had revealed and promptly burst into tears. Timothy remained still and silent…

*** *

Nobody noticed the half-grown youth as he walked briskly across the neatly manicured lawns toward the austere, red brick building on the far side of the campus. The continuous rain had kept most of the remaining inhabitants indoors and apart from a few dejected looking guardsmen, the garrison was to all intents and purposes, deserted.

Thus, nobody noticed as he approached the old oak door and pushed back the hood of his coat as he pressed the doorbell. His blonde curls provided a glimmer of light in this dull and oppressive place. Almost instantly it seemed, the door creaked heavily open and the slight figure slipped through and into the shelter the old house offered.

Harold Stanton dozed in his customary leather chair beside the meagre fire which failed miserably to warm the enormous room. Sunk in his personal mire of unaccustomed emotions, his reverie was rudely interrupted when a soft voice spoke, close to his ear.

"Sir?" The sergeant's eyes flickered open, "Sir…" the urgency in the word caused Harold to pull himself up straighter in the chair and peer short-sightedly at the intruder. He reached for his spectacles and methodically replaced them on his nose before his response acknowledged both that he had heard the enquiry and that he was indeed Sergeant Stanton. "Sergeant Stanton to you boy!" he barked, "and just what the devil do you think you're doing here in my study?" His embarrassment at being caught dozing gave an increased sharpness to his tone, "No one enters unannounced! Who let you in?" he added for good measure.

"Forgive me for disturbing you," ignoring the question, the soft voice continued, "but I need you to understand something." Now this was a departure from the usual reason for intrusion into his private space. It was more common for visitors to want something from him, at least, something more practical than understanding. He was intrigued in spite of himself and in any case, he had no idea who this very young man could be. For a moment his slowing mental processes provided a pause whilst he tried to gather his wits and make sense of what he perceived.

"I don't want to rush you, Sir, but I don't have much time," the boy spoke again.

"But who are you?"

"It doesn't matter who I am; it only matters what I need to give to you." Again the ambivalent reply confused Harry and he struggled to comprehend as he considered the possibility that he was actually dreaming. But no, he could feel the meagre warmth emanating from his fireplace and he could see the small figure of the youth beside him; his blonde curls and bright blue eyes seeming almost infantile although the streak of mud on his cheek and the suggestion of muscles beginning to fill out his arms and legs belied his youth.

"Sir?" again the boy spoke, his voice reflecting his urgency as the volume slightly increased.

"Yes boy, I'm listening." The gruff response was accompanied by Harold pulling himself yet more upright in the chair and leaning forward so as to better hear the child. "But you need to tell me how you came to be here; who sent you? What do you want?"

"Wait and you will understand." The response was unsatisfactory but for now it would have to suffice since no other explanation was forthcoming.

"You have two sons," he began.

"One son," Harry corrected, "and he's not much use to anyone anymore!" bitterness was evident in his tone. Ignoring the rebuff, the young visitor continued, "Your sons need you to hear what I have to say." Harry leaned back in his chair; eyes closed, and resigned himself to listening to this extraordinary apparition.

"Sometimes things happen in our lives about which we can do nothing but accept the truth in what has occurred. We may not like or want the outcome we are presented with but we have to face it and deal with it in order to be able to move on with our lives. This is true even when we think we are nearing the end of our time here because it is not for us to know the exact moment of our ultimate demise. Until that moment, life goes on and lessons are still to be learned." Harry grunted disgruntledly and waved his hand indicating that the boy should get a move on with his tale, or message or whatever it was.

Timothy moved closer to the old man's chair and placed his young hand carefully on the back of Harry's old gnarled knuckles. "Be patient," he calmed, and he felt the hand beneath his own twitch and flex before it began to relax, "I have not come to chastise you, nor to tell you what you should do. I come to guide and suggest; the choices have always been yours. It was your choices that took you from your sons while they were still young, it was your choice to favour one son above the other, it was because of your choices that both of your sons rebelled and went their various ways. And finally, it was by your choices that one of your sons is no longer here on earth and that the other needs you more now than ever before."

Tears trickled slowly down Captain Stanton's wrinkled cheeks as he recognised the truth in what this child was telling him. The boy continued, "I do not say these things to hurt you nor to condemn, I know that you did what you thought right at the time, and that is all that anyone can do. But it would be a foolish man indeed who did not take an opportunity to make amends were it offered to him as I am offering it to you."

"What must I do?"

"Dad," Jay's voice was instantly recognisable and Harry sat up with a start. "Dad, don't speak, just listen. I went to see Tomo. He's in a pretty bad way. Not physically but emotionally. He feels he's let the side down. Failed in his duty to you and he thinks he has nothing of value left to live for. Go to him Dad. Show him that he is worth a million of me. I wasted what chances I had and look what happened to me eh? Well I've been given this chance to put things right for Tomo, so here I am and now it's up to you. Don't leave it too long old thing, he needs you now."

"Jay, don't go..." but the fire burned lower and the light outside faded and the room grew darker and darker...

***

Vera, the house matron, bustled into the room, snapping on the electric light as she closed the door sharply behind her. Harold woke with a start and found himself staring at a single white rose balanced precariously on a small brown-paper parcel which lay beside his pipe and tobacco tin on the table by his chair. Automatically he picked up the rose and sniffed its delicate, though exquisite, perfume. Laying it aside and after a pensive moment or two, he took the lightweight parcel and carefully untied the string in order to reveal the item therein. Soon, in his palm, lay a green plastic soldier. A one legged soldier, to be precise, and one which supported itself on a cocktail stick crutch that had been carefully crafted and glued in place in order for the soldier to stand tall with the rest of his plastic regiment; his pride and honour intact instead of having been cast unceremoniously into a rubbish bin.

Chapter Eighteen

It had been a long hard struggle but finally she had made it! The graduation ceremony had been brief and she wondered whether the occasion had actually warranted the hours of agonising over her outfit, makeup and hairstyle and the inordinate amount of time she had spent in getting it all just right. She smiled to herself as she turned the key in the ancient oak door that creaked ominously open, reminding her of the horror film she had enjoyed last week. As soon as she turned on the light the atmosphere changed and the warm glow of the orange shaded lamp and burgundy drapes welcomed her home. Colourful scatter cushions and throws adorned the saggy old sofa and burnt out candles dripped their solidified wax onto the marble hearth. It was late but she would have just one celebratory drink to finish off what had been a satisfying day before retiring for a long sleep after the tensions of the previous few weeks.

Sandra had found it hard to make the change from dependency to independence. The loss of her parents, whom she had so resented in her teenage years, had made her reassess her life and attitude to ambition and her future. No longer did she have the protection of their hard work and loving support. No longer could she behave in the wild and childishly selfish ways that had become habitual and which had been accepted by her unwise parents through their doting on their beloved daughter. She realised that she had thrown away several opportunities and had made some very unwise choices.

She regretted her previous unkindness and demanding of Tom as well as her summary dismissal of his concern for her future; where was he now? Why did he not respond to her attempts to contact him? He never replied to text messages or email and she had no idea where he had gone after the house had been sold. Once he had been sure that she had somewhere to live, money in the bank and an opportunity to make a career for herself, he had just packed up and left on his bike, waving a dismissive hand and calling out, "See ya!" Perhaps he thought she was still trying to inveigle her way into his heart? But no, she would just like to feel that she had some family to support her and to share things with. There were times when she was exceedingly lonely; real friends were hard to come by and even harder to keep!

One person who had stood by her and who never judged nor criticised but who was mysterious and elusive at times, was Bethany. The unlikely duo had become firm friends although on somewhat unequal terms. It was not the usual sort of friendship where, if there was a need for advice or just a friendly chat, one could pick up the phone and call at any hour of the day or night and Bethany was more of a mentor than a close confidante. Sandra often realised that she knew very little of Bethany's life apart from where their paths crossed and as she sat sipping her Irish coffee, the warmth of the alcohol softening the hard protective shell she had built around her feelings, she determined to invite Bethany to visit more often, perhaps to take a short break together. It might be a nice way to thank her for all her support over the last few years and there was no doubt that without her, Sandra would have floundered and probably sunk into a mire of depression and despondency.

Tipping her head back and downing the last of the creamy beverage, Sandra wearily, and a little unsteadily, made her way up the creaky stairs to the small bedroom above. As she glanced into the chilly bathroom, she shivered and decided she would shower and cleanse herself in the morning. For now she flopped onto the bohemian styled bed, with its gaudy and lacy drapes and pillows. She pulled the soft quilt around her still fully dressed body and just as her eyes were closing, she remembered that she did not know how to contact Bethany. All she had was a slip of paper on which was written, 'Call me'. Somehow the elusive, austere but caring lady always managed to materialise, just when Sandra needed her most.

Dreamily she relived the first time she had met Bethany on the bus to college after the awful fiasco with her wayward hair. The second meeting had been on that miserable day of the funeral, but it was the third that had been most surprising…

***

It was a hot afternoon, in fact the hottest day he could remember and the coolness of the pool sent tingles down his spine. Thomas sat under the shade of the big willow tree, his whitest of white skin protected not only by the shadows but also by half a jar of sun screen. He watched as Timothy splashed about in the shallow water, sometimes boyishly pretending to be a shark and at others trying to catch the myriad of minnows that wove their way through the softly swaying reeds just under the surface of the sparkling water. He had long forgotten to be jealous of Timothy's lithe, athletic movements and tanned, healthy skin. Indeed he revelled in Timothy's beauty in an asexual and simply artistic admiration. Through his friend he could experience things that would otherwise be lost from him; his own shapeless, bulbous body, grown more ungainly with adolescence, forgotten in his pleasure in sharing Timothy's enjoyment.

Always guarded and careful to watch for signs of Timothy's malady, Thomas had appointed himself unofficial observer. He shared this role with the ageing Snowball who neither saw nor heard as well as he had when the boys were younger. Nevertheless, the two were diligent in their task and had guided and sheltered Timothy through a dwindling number of incidents. As Timothy grew into a young man, so his seizures had lessened both in quantity and in severity. Generally he was fit, healthy and able to live a full, normal life which included sport and play in equal measure. The triggers for his petit mal were erratic and not fully understood by the medics but they were unilaterally of the opinion that stressful times, such as changes in environment, sudden excitement or deep sadness were the most likely to initiate a 'funny turn' as Carrie liked to term the fits. Thus it was that a combination of these factors culminated in an unfortunate circumstance wherein Thomas watched with increasing agitation as Timothy failed to resurface after a particularly spectacular dive from a rock into the deepest part of the pool. Having watched Timothy make a similar entrance to the water on numerous occasions, Thomas knew to count to about forty five before seeing the blonde head reappear further downstream. After sixty five he rose awkwardly to his feet. At ninety, he stumbled to the water's edge and peered expectantly at the rippled surface...

Suddenly, a loud crash resounded through the shrubs and undergrowth, a flash of yellow and grey and a violent splash as someone dived into the water, made Thomas cry out with alarm and he sat down almost as abruptly as he had scrambled to his feet.

A few seconds later an older woman, fully clothed, scrambled up the bank carrying in her arms the unconscious body of Timothy. With total disregard for her own bedraggled state, she laid him face down on the grass and began to massage his back to expel the water he had inhaled. Satisfied that he was no longer in danger of drowning, she placed him carefully in the recovery position and then turned her attention to Thomas. The lad was petrified and completely unable to utter a single word.

"Do you have a mobile phone?" she asked.

"Yyy-yes," he nodded and clumsily handed it to her; no more capable of making a call than he was of speaking.

"Can you go and get me some towels and a blanket from the house over there?"

In answer Thomas lumbered to his feet and began to run awkwardly to fetch more help. Soon Carrie and Elsa, carrying blankets and towels, came running across the meadow, while Eleanor followed a little more sedately bringing a flask and some dry clothes for the stranger.

Having established that Timothy was alive, if not kicking, the four women waited for an ambulance to arrive. Although it was almost certainly just another seizure and already he was showing signs of recovery, there was always a possibility that Timothy had banged his head or breathed in rather more water than was good for him and so it was agreed that the paramedics should take him and Eleanor to A&E and that the stranger, who had suffered a few minor cuts and grazes, should accompany them. The family would follow in the big Range Rover so that they had a vehicle in which to return home later.

***

The quiet bleeping of the monitor punctuated the silence of the private room in which Timothy slept. She checked the drip, adjusted the monitor, gently straightened the blankets and felt his pulse. Satisfied that all was well, she turned to tiptoe out of the room. On reaching the door she heard a small sound and whipped her head around to see, much to her surprise, Timothy looking straight at her. His wide blue eyes looked straight into her soul and he smiled.

"You've come a long way," he said, "and you've further to go but you're on the right path and you're learning fast. Don't give up now will you?"

How did he know how close she had come to throwing in the towel, to giving up this venture? A nursing degree sounded easy enough but it was far from straightforward and time and again she had wanted to walk away from it all. And who was he anyway? There was something about him; his demeanour, his hair, his eyes, which reminded her of someone she had seen a long time ago...

She recognised instantly the tall grey haired woman who stood by his bedside.

"Bethany!" she gasped, "How... I mean where... I... what on earth are you doing here?" Bethany smiled her quixotic and enigmatic smile and replied, "We've come to make sure you don't undo all that we have done for you! You always were impulsive and sometimes you still fail to recognise what is the right thing for you to do! Timothy and I need to tell you something but you must listen and not question until you have heard the whole. Will you do that?"

Chapter Nineteen

Dora puffed as she clambered up the last few steps of the rocky path and breathed a sigh of relief as she rounded the final bend and the old cottage came into view. She was getting too old for these arduous scrambles! Too old? She laughed silently to herself; she could never be too old now... It always surprised her to find the stone dwelling nestled into the cliff as though it was cut out of the rock itself, its low slate roof seemed to be alive as a thin line of breath-like smoke snaked its way from the chimney into the almost cloudless sky. She tapped lightly on the door and without waiting for a response, pushed it open and stepped into the timeless and welcoming room.

Old Bess was nowhere to be seen but the inevitable conglomeration of cats; more numerous than ever, were somnolently draped everywhere. Some lifted a sleepy head and gazed mournfully at the newcomer, some rose to their feet and arched their backs before resuming their slumber, one meowed pitifully, its tail gently twitching and another, unseen by Dora, slipped silently out of the open window and disappeared from view. Dora took the old kettle and filled it before placing it carefully on the hob in readiness for the cup of tea that would surely be offered as soon as her hostess returned.

Before long Old Bess came bustling in, closely followed by Daniel and, again unseen, by the same small cat that had hurried out to announce Dora's arrival.

"Welcome, welcome my dear!" exclaimed the sage, "Daniel has been filling me in on the success of your work with Sally. I'm so pleased she is recovered and so grateful for your interference. She is a deserving case and none better than you two to put her straight. Besides," she added with a finger to the side of her nose and a twinkle in her eye, "there was also the important matter of young Tom to consider!"

"It was our pleasure to be sure." Dora smiled at Bess before greeting Daniel with a warm embrace, "We gained far more from helping the sweet girl than she ever received from us, didn't we dear?" She beamed at her husband and in return he, lip quivering and eyes watering, unable to speak, squeezed her hand; the ageless, timeless love between the two of them was evident in his eyes and in his whole demeanour.

Later, when tea had been supped and bellies filled with sweetmeats and cakes, Old Bess leaned back in her rocking chair. The fire had burned low and the light had faded from outside the windows; two cats vied for the most comfortable place on her ample lap and she sighed deeply before speaking in a low voice. As she gently rocked, in a sing song tone she explained.

"Your work is done and the time has come for you to leave this place. Wait…" she raised her hand as Dora began to protest, "No one can stay for ever. There are other places for you to be and other experiences to be had. You have been fortunate to have had this extra time. Maybe you will continue together, I don't know, that is not for me to dictate but I do know that you have completed this part of your journey. Soon he will be here and you will go." She rose to her feet and crossed to stand between the two aging lovers. Taking Daniel's hand she placed it in her own and ceremoniously raised it to her lips and kissed it before placing it in Dora's frail and wrinkled palm. She held both their hands in her own and commanded them, "Close your eyes." Her imperious tone brooked no argument and she continued, "Know that you have put right the wrongs that occurred in your lifetime. Daniel was taken too soon and your girls, Jen and Tam, suffered as a result of your depths of despair and desolation. There was no blame to be laid but a price to be paid. Your debt is cleared, your daughters have gone before you and they await you in the great beyond."

As she spoke the room began to spin with smoky vapours, ephemeral figures whispered and whirled, focuses blurred and all sensations became disparate and indistinguishable one from another. The scene

93

dissolved into dust and a light wind blew the particles into the darkening atmosphere. A black figure floated into the darkness, his piercing blue eyes the only discernible evidence of his being, and with arms spread wide he gathered into his voluminous cloak all the swirling nothingness and was gone.

***

The light of a new dawn crept over the window sill and into the silence of the empty room. There; perfectly formed in its pearly white iridescence, exquisitely perfumed and nestling at its heart, a solitary diamond dewdrop; lay a single rose.

***

Despite her new found contentment, Sally was troubled. She wasn't at all sure that she was ready to meet this girl. She had heard so much about her wildness and her unreasonable demands, her almost heartless response to the death of her parents and her total lack of interest in her cousin's welfare, that she had almost made up her mind to hate her before she had even met the woman. Woman? Was she a woman now? She had sounded mature enough on the telephone, but it was hard to tell these days and her manner had been somewhat abrupt. "I need to see Tom," she had begun; no preamble, no niceties, just a demand. She had softened a little when Sally had agreed that she had the right number and that Tom would meet her at the station next Saturday. And it was possible that she had heard a little sob of relief just before the phone call ended. But still she felt uncomfortable and was nervously agitated about the whole business.

***

Tom waited, involuntarily wringing his cap in his hands as his eyes flicked repeatedly to above the station entrance where, suspended, was a large round clock whose hands slipped slowly, inexorably toward the scheduled time of arrival. How long had it been? He thought back. They had parted company not long after his Aunt and

Uncle's affairs had been settled. Although they had been obliged to meet once or twice with solicitors to sign some official papers, the last time he had seen her had been to witness the placing and blessing of a simple headstone; a ceremony that had left them saddened and not knowing what to say to one another. It had seemed such an empty end to a mutually unfortunate chapter in their lives. Since that bleak occasion he had not seen or heard from his cousin. He knew neither where she was nor what she was doing or how she was supporting herself. Slight pangs of guilt washed over him as he realised he had neglected his one remaining family member and as his eyes flicked once again to the clock, he resolved to be more attentive in the future.

Would he recognise her? How should he greet her? What would they talk about? Surely there was precious little that they had in common now? His thoughts wandered to Sally and a smile twitched the corners of his mouth. She had become his family, his rock and his whole world. Mutually supportive of each other they were a team, a unit and their strength lay in their togetherness and their loyalty; their love.

It was a strange union and one which neither had looked for nor expected. For Sally it was a constant surprise to find herself waking cradled in the crook of Tom's strong arm and she often pinched herself to make sure she wasn't still dreaming. She treasured their intimate moments, having resigned herself many years before to spinsterhood and a lonely old age. She was amazed and delighted at the change in her circumstances and although at forty one she was nine years older than her lover, his maturity was greater than hers and he led her through the maze of love and life. They learned together, played together and worked together. There had been no mention of formalising their situation but they were both secure in the knowledge that they had committed themselves to each other and that they were where they should be, where they were meant to be and that although in time things may change, right now their life together seemed perfect.

Tom was still smiling to himself as the rushing sound of an approaching train broke into his reverie and the squealing of the slowing diesel engine's brakes heralded the arrival of his cousin.

***

Sandra gazed unseeing out of the carriage window. The clickety-clack rhythm of wheels on rails had lulled her into a sleepy trance and her thoughts wandered from her mild anxiety about the forthcoming reunion with Tom to the strange series of events that had led her onto this path of reconciliation. The day that Bethany had come to her with that young man who had almost drowned had been one full of surprises. She'd never really thought much about her life; she lived from day to day, hand to mouth and just accepted things that happened without questioning her purpose. Soon after her parent's funeral, in an attempt to provide her with a sense of direction, Bethany had suggested that she should take up nursing and she very much enjoyed her work. She smiled as she thought of the certificate proudly framed and displayed on her bedroom wall.

She'd even cleared away some of her clutter in order that it might be more clearly seen each time she entered the room. And now, following the unexpected and surprise meeting on that fateful day, she knew that there was a greater reason for her being and although she had not fully understood all that Bethany had explained to her, she accepted that she had to make her peace with Tom before she could move forward with her destiny. Not that she knew what that future should be but she trusted Bethany as did the young lad whose bright blue eyes had haunted her ever since. Her hand went involuntarily to the package in her coat pocket. The beautiful white rose bud that the boy had given her, now preserved in an acrylic bubble, was her gift to Tom and Sally. A paperweight; unique in its design and exquisite in its execution, she hoped they would appreciate her peace offering.

"Go to Tom," Bethany had said, "make your peace and then your path will become clear. Things happen for reasons; every small thing that

96

you do is like throwing a pebble into a pond. The ripples will spread far and wide as your choices affect the actions of others; action and reaction in an ever perpetuating motion."

***

And so here she was, snapping out of her reverie as the rhythm of the rails slowed and the train drew into the station. And there was Tom, waiting for her just as he had done so many times before.

Chapter Twenty

The long lazy summer was slipping inexorably into autumn. Eleanor pulled up the collar of her cosy cardigan and shoved her hands deep into the pockets where her fingers felt a folded paper, the contents of which had filled her thoughts for the best part of the day. It was time to make a move. Her aging bones grumbled as she rose awkwardly to her feet. Taking her cane from its resting place against the wrought iron table, she slowly and haltingly made her way down the garden path from the gazebo to the large conservatory that adorned the back of the house. Once inside she paused to absorb the warmth of the windless sunroom and made a mental note to herself to look out her winter coat before venturing into the garden again this year.

"Ah! There you are!" Elsa smiled at the older woman, "I was just coming to see whether you are ready for your tea? Carrie has been baking and she's anxious for you to take the first bite of her offerings." Elsa winked conspiratorially at Eleanor as she took her elbow and guided her through to the lounge where the coffee table was set for afternoon tea. Fine porcelain cups and saucers were almost a thing of the past since most people seemed content to sup from heavier, clumsy, mugs, but Eleanor was 'old school' and she appreciated quality, etiquette and the time and trouble such things took. Elsa and Rosa were happy to indulge her whims and, truth to tell, the tea tasted so much better in the fine chinaware.

"Is Rosa joining us today?" Eleanor enquired and was secretly pleased when the answer came in the negative. Not that she wanted to avoid her step-daughter-in-law, but she needed some time to herself in order to get to grips with this puzzle with which she had been presented.

"She's away on some business until Friday night," replied Elsa as she poured a cup of tea for the older lady. "I thought I might take the opportunity to spring clean her rooms," she continued, "unless you have something you'd like me to do for you?"

"No, no, I think that's a good idea."

A resounding crash from the kitchen, followed by a woeful wail, interrupted the conversation and Elsa sprang to her feet and hurriedly left the room to find out what was the problem.

Eleanor once again fingered the paper in her pocket and a frown furrowed her already wrinkled brow. She wasn't sure what to make of the contents of the letter that had arrived in the post a day earlier. She had been pondering the conundrum ever since she had slit open the manila envelope and slid out the heavy sheet of paper which was embossed with an official looking lawyer's crest. With a sigh she rearranged her face into her customary calm expression which quickly became a smile as a somewhat tearful Carrie came cautiously into the room carefully carrying a small plate of fairy cakes. "Oh my, those look delicious!" she exclaimed as Carrie, sniffing mightily, proffered the plate. "My made more," she mumbled, "but my dropped 'em!"

"Well, there are plenty left for us to eat!" soothed Eleanor as she bit into the surprisingly tasty offering. Carrie smiled a watery grimace and a few minutes later Snowball shuffled into the room. His lip licking and the few sticky crumbs adorning his whiskers bore witness to the clearing up operation he had just performed. "Goo' boy!" muttered Carrie.

***

Later that same night, as she lay back in her bed, comfortably propped up by the many pillows that eased her night-time breathing, Eleanor once more took out the letter. She had not thought of Phillip for many, many years. Her sister's former husband had more or less disappeared from her memory and it was with a slight shock and a sense of the surreal that she read his name in the missive she had received. He must be quite old by now? She smiled wryly to herself as she realised that she too was a good age; where did the years go? What could he possible want with the family now? Jen, her sister, had died an untimely death a long time ago and her daughter, Tam, had also been dead now for several years. Nevertheless, there was always a pang of grief when Eleanor thought on her niece and adopted daughter and an inevitable tear threatened to spill onto the page. What cruel twist of fate had decided that she should also die so young? She paused; eyes closed, and took a deep breath, before once more perusing the words:

Dear Mrs Taylor,

> *I write to you on behalf of your former brother-in-law, Phillip Baxter, who has asked me to confirm that you are willing and able to make arrangements to travel to his home in Minchington where he has some important information to impart to you concerning one Thomas Pearce who it is believed currently resides at your home.*
> *Mr Baxter, who is unable to travel to you since he is bedridden and requires constant care and medication, is anxious to discuss with you matters referring to the formality of any continuing agreement.*
> *Please reply to this letter in the first instance confirming that you are able to meet his request upon receipt of which affirmation I will contact you again to provide you with further details concerning this matter.*

Yours faithfully,

John Forrester, LLB, LPC, GDL, MSc, BSc

Quite apart from the bizarre lack of punctuation which makes all lawyer's letters so difficult to understand, Eleanor was baffled by the reference to Thomas. He had lived with them for what seemed like forever and by now had become an intrinsic member of the family. No one thought of him as a visitor; indeed no one, not even he, had

100

mentioned his mother, his home or his leaving them for several years now. She couldn't imagine him not being at home with them all and certainly Timothy depended on him for all sorts of reasons. It was a mutual dependency since Thomas's health issues prevented him from taking part in many outdoor activities which meant that he was able to watch Timothy and be on hand to alert the family should he fit and need assistance. In this way he felt that he was a part of Timothy's life and was able to participate in theory if not in practise. No one knew the rules of Amateur Rugby League better than he did! So far Timothy's petit mal had not been a dangerously debilitating problem; nevertheless it did need to be taken seriously in order that he should come to no harm whenever he was stricken.

Eleanor pulled her wandering thoughts back to the current issue and considered the odd request. It would not be easy for her to travel to Minchington. Although her mobility was moderately good for an elderly woman, she was slow and she no longer drove herself. Either she would need to ask someone to take her or else the journey would involve a complicated series of buses, taxis and trains. Above all, she was curious. She would have to respond and hope that the 'further details' would clarify the situation. She closed her eyes as she decided that perhaps Elsa would be the best person to ask… or maybe Shane? She also determined not to mention the letter or its contents to Simon or Rosa and definitely not to the boys; not until she had a better idea what this was all about.

Chapter Twenty-One

He had long since stopped asking why. There were no answers. It wasn't fair, but then he remembered his mother saying over and over again, in response to his protests, that no one ever promised that life would be fair.

As he lay in the bed that had been positioned near the window, the same bed that his mother had lain in the last time he had seen her alive, he gazed out over the Autumnal garden. The reddish gold leaves had fallen, carpeting the lawn in their lush deep-pile glory and the sun glinted on the tops of the remaining bare branches that still bore the last of the over ripened fruits that clung desperately to them. They would fall; the next time a breeze shook their safe harbour, they would inevitably fall, thudding onto the wet lawn, splitting as they landed and scattering their white flesh over the grass. The birds would peck lazily, already gorged on the bounteous harvest and the remnants would rot into the ground, providing fresh nutrition for next year's crop.

Damn this disease! Damn this dependency! Damn everything. Why couldn't he be as his mother had been? Gracious and forgiving in her final days, she had eased his pain at her passing. She had blessed him and Heather, his sister who had borne the brunt of the burden of care for their mother's final demise. She had died at peace with the world and those she loved but he…? He was angry! He was so angry that he thought he might burst of anger. Why? Everything that he had ever held dear, everything that he had ever wanted, everything he had ever tried to achieve had been taken from him and now his life was ebbing away and he was helpless to change anything. All he was able to do, it seemed, was to rant and rail at life's iniquities. Well, he was damned if he was going to lie here and die quietly! There were things he needed to put right before he left this world. He rang the bell by his bedside and waited impatiently for Nurse Eliza to appear.

Eliza had been good to him. He knew he didn't show his appreciation for all that she unquestioningly did for him. At first Heather had nursed him but she was no longer a young woman and it wasn't fair of him to expect her to give up the life she had made for herself after their mother had died. She loved the little business she had created. Hand crafted gifts and trinkets that she worked on all winter and which she sold at markets and fairs in the summer months. It wasn't that she needed money; Mother had provided generously for both of them, but the satisfaction of seeing her work appreciated and desired, filled her heart and gave purpose to her life.

She had come willingly when he was first diagnosed with terminal bone cancer and she did her best to provide the care he needed, despite the fact that he was fiercely reluctant to accept any help. When it became obvious that he was going to need more than she could give, she found Eliza. Where and how she came was a mystery to Phillip but he was happy to accept the ministrations of this enigmatic woman who came and went almost unseen. Her efficiency and capability astonished him.

She came silently into the room. She carefully plumped up the pillows and smoothed the counterpane before checking the morphine drip. When she was assured that all was as it should be, she was ready to respond to his request for paper and a pen. She would post the letter he dictated when she took Bouncer for his walk later that afternoon. Little brown Bouncer had come with Eliza and he followed her wherever she went; never needing a leash he shadowed her every move. He was her confidante and companion and the only time he was not at her heels was when he was curled at the foot of Phillip's bed; perhaps when she was bathing or shopping.

The wind swirled the leaves around her feet and Bouncer almost disappeared in the piles that he was determined were harbouring some small creature that needed exterminating. Living up to his name he bounced down the lane scattering the fallen vegetation and barking excitedly at invisible monsters. Eliza posted the letter in the bright red box on the corner of the village and, calling Bouncer to heel, walked on to the small café in the middle of the High Street. The door slammed closed behind her as the wind whipped at her scarf. She ordered herself a cup of hot chocolate and relaxed in the warmth of the cosy room. Bouncer was tucked under the table; his presence a concession to his good behaviour. She knew that she did not have long in this place. Phillip was deteriorating faster than he realised; she did not disillusion him when he talked of next year or even next month. Heather also knew but she too would not reveal the truth to her brother. At the age of seventy nine he'd had a good innings. He'd done some bad things and made some catastrophic mistakes in his life but good had come from it too. Jen and Tam for a start; although their paths had not been easy, many positive things had come from their existence. And now the truth was to be revealed about that other life he had created. What would come from this revelation? Eliza breathed deeply, blew on her hot beverage and closed her eyes. "Make it good," she murmured and Bouncer stirred and sighed at her feet. "All will be well," he seemed to say.

***

The news came a few days later. The official looking envelope lay on the hall carpet and she picked it up as she made her way to the kitchen to make the morning coffee. The lady would come! She knew without opening the letter that Eleanor would come. Phillip would have time. That had been her greatest concern; that time would run out for the poor man. Then she laughed at herself; of course he would have time! Wasn't that precisely why she was here? To make sure that he had time and that this time was used wisely. Sometimes she wondered at her own forgetfulness. Old Bess had reassured her, hadn't she?

***

Disbelief, shock, astonishment and curiosity had oscillated through his whole being. At any moment one fleeting feeling was deposed in favour of an even more troubling thought. How could it be? Was it true? Why announce this bombshell now? And what a crazy way to

104

make such a preposterous claim. Nevertheless, there it was in black and white. Just a few short sentences, boxed in and bold, ensuring that the eye would be caught and the words read. Oh, he had read the words alright – but the largeness of implication therein belied the diminutiveness of the disproportionate messenger.

Was it pure chance that he had read that particular page? He usually skimmed through the sports section, discarded the property news and classified ads, removed the television guide and perused more carefully the rest of the local paper to ascertain whether there was anything newsworthy to note. On this occasion the births and deaths announcements happened to be on the back page of the classified ad section and as he clumsily fumbled with the oversized newspaper, it slipped to the floor; back page uppermost:

> *"With apologies for the long delay in making it public, Lucy Pearce and Phillip Baxter are delighted to announce the birth of their daughter Catherine Louise."*

It was the name that caught his eye. He had not thought of his former lady friend for many years. Indeed he had lost contact with her soon after he realised that her loyalties were divided between him and the many other men that came and went. At the same time he had returned home to find his mother sick and dying and had never left Minchington again. He picked up the paper and scrutinised it for more details; but there were none. No date, time or weight such as might usually be found in a birth announcement notification. Obviously, there must be some mistake. Perhaps it was another Phillip Baxter? It played on his mind that it was surely too much of a coincidence for both names to be the same? Straight away he decided to investigate further.

The girl on the end of the phone was quite sure that the request to publish the notice had been sent by post and assured Phillip that she would find the file and forward to him any information that she was entitled to give out. In due course, she called back saying that the payment cheque was signed; L. Pearce and she gave the name of the bank from whom the cheque had been issued. There was no letter, no address, no name; just a scrap of paper requesting that the words should be printed exactly as written. "I'm sorry I can't help you further," she sympathised and rang off.

Although this had been upsetting enough, it had been the second announcement that caused Phillip a major trauma. Once again, the following week, the paper curiously opened on the births and deaths announcement page and prompted by his previous surprise, he swiftly scanned the columns. Of course he hadn't expected to find anything else. Unless someone was playing a tremendous hoax; and who would do such a thing, surely it was just a coincidence? But it rankled with his reasoning and hadn't his mother always told him that there is no such thing as coincidence? Strangely he was not surprised to find it but its content astonished and terrified him. He read:

> Born to Cathy Louise Pearce; a son, Thomas Baxter Pearce. Mother and son are well.

Nothing more. Just as before, it was a simple announcement without details or any indication of time or date. One might assume the event was recent but then again...

Chapter Twenty-Two

The insistent banging on the door brought Eliza scurrying down the stairs, pulling her flimsy housecoat over her nightdress in an attempt to retain a little of the warmth that she had left behind in her bed. Who on earth could it be at this time in the morning?

She did not recognise the shabbily dressed woman who stood shivering on the doorstep but her naturally compassionate nature kept her irritation at bay as she enquired as to how she could help the lady.

"Is 'e in?" The gruff voice bore witness to a heavy smoker.

"Do you mean Mr Baxter?"

"Yes, 'im." The terse response did not bode well for niceties and Eliza bristled in spite of her gentleness.

"Yes he is here, but I'm afraid you are much too early to see him. Can you come back a little later?"

"I'll wait," and she made her way towards the wrought iron bench that was placed near the front door, under the porch roof.

"Oh dear me, no! It's much too cold for you to sit out here. You'd better come in and I'll find you a cup of tea or something if you'd like that." Without replying the newcomer pushed through the open door and waited in the dim hallway for Eliza to indicate which of the many wooden panelled doors she should use. Before long the somewhat unkempt and odorous lady was seated at the kitchen table cradling a steaming mug of coffee. She took out a pack of cigarettes and lit one while Eliza hurriedly opened a window and found a saucer to act as an ash tray. Already she could tell that this was going to be an unusual morning.

Excusing herself, and with a slight pang of concern at leaving this stranger alone in her kitchen, she hurriedly returned to her room to dress before waking her patient and informing him of his visitor.

The usual and essential routine of medication, ablutions and a light breakfast were completed, and after almost a whole pack of cigarettes had been consumed by the abider in the kitchen, the stranger was ushered into Phillip's room.

**

The story that she told was fantastical; unbelievable, and yet he instinctively knew it was true.

"I didn't know where you were, so's I couldn'' 'ave told yer," she began, "I got 'ome from me night job and there you was, gone." By the time she had divested herself of her shabby coat and unwrapped the woollen scarf from its several layers wound round her head, Phillip could begin to see a vague likeness to the woman with whom he had once shared his bed and, on occasions, his home. As he listened to her crackling voice he found himself wondering what on earth he had seen in her. Had he seen anything or was it one of his drink induced infatuations which had depended on his need for her flesh rather than herself. Her once lustrous brown hair was now thin, straggly and bleached blonde. Her skin had similarly suffered from a surfeit of tobacco and alcohol. Her former well defined features were now heavily lined and the bright red lipstick and blue eye shadow did nothing to enhance her looks. Her back was bowed and she walked with the steady plod of one who spent more time treading the streets than is commonplace. Instinctively he felt a brief pang of pity but it was quickly dismissed as memories flooded in and her story unfolded.

"I'd told you many times that I'd got a little job cleanin' after hours at the supermarket down the road. I knew yer were'n' listenin', you was too far down in yer own dumps to be bothered about mine.

108

Anyway, I'd 'ad an inklin' I were up the duff before that mornin' when you'd scarpered. I'd bin down the quack's the day before an' 'ad to go back for me results. So I went, and I was; pregnant that is. At first I fought I'd 'ave ter get rid of it but I wanted ter try an' find you first. Y'know, jus' to let yer know you might 'ave a kid. I'd've married yer if yer'd asked me!" Here she grinned a hideous, almost toothless grimace and he inwardly shuddered at the thought. Eliza, who was perched discreetly on the end of the window seat, watching her patient for signs of distress, saw his eyes close briefly as he attempted to shut out the abhorrent thought.

"Anyways," Lucy continued, "I tried to find out where yer'd gone; you 'adn't left much in the way of clues, but then you never 'ad much did yer?" The question didn't warrant an answer although at that moment Phillip realised he'd actually had everything he needed but he'd thrown it all away; his wife, his daughter, his sister, his home. And for what? For this woman? He shuddered again and opened his eyes and tried to smile at her in encouragement to continue her tale.

"Well, to cut a long story short, I couldn' find yer and by the time I'd stopped tryin' I was too far gone for an abortion. So I 'ad 'er. She were a bonny babe, full o' smiles and gurgles. I was lucky to be taken in by one o' them unwed mothers' hostels so she an' I lived there for nigh on five years. Then I got a job an' rented a little flat, she wen' ter school and that's when we found out that she were a bit simple like. Nothing bad enough for 'er to be taken from me or put in a mental thingy, but I 'ad to watch 'er 'cause she was like to wander off an' get lost. She couldn't always remember like other kids do. They called 'er 'Come 'ome Cathy' 'cause I was always out lookin' for 'er. I called 'er Cathy after your sister Kate; you tol' me about 'er once, y'know, the one what died? An' then Louise after me mam." She paused to sniff back a theatrical tear at the mention of her mother and Eliza realised the degree to which this woman was playing on the weakened emotional state of her former lover. Phillip however, was unmoved by the dramatic performance and perfunctorily proffered a tissue box. Instead of taking one, she rummaged in her capacious bag and, after a few minutes, produced a tatty wallet from which she withdrew a faded and much thumbed photograph. "There she is!" she exclaimed and waved the picture toward Phillip.

The likeness was extraordinary. Looking out at him, with a sunny smile, was a young girl who bore an uncanny resemblance to his sister, Heather. He studied the picture for a few moments before offering it to Eliza; unwittingly drawing her into the discussion. She stepped forward and instinctively adjusted his pillows and checked the morphine drip before taking the scruffy piece of paper. She looked at Phillip in surprise and her eyes silently questioned him; should she fetch Heather? He gave a slight shake of his head and turned back to Lucy who was blowing her nose on a grubby cotton handkerchief.

Stuffing the slightly soggy fabric into her pocket, she resumed the story. "It were all a long time ago now, an' I don' 'old any grudges. You weren' there an' I was so I did what I 'ad ter do. She were mostly a good girl until she was near growed up. Then it 'appened. She were raped." Another dramatic pause ensued for effect, which was indeed forthcoming. Phillip jerked upright and Eliza immediately took his arm defensively protecting the medical equipment to which he was attached. She eased him back onto the pillows and quickly offered to make coffee for them all.

"Yeah, I need a fag an' I don' s'pose you'll want me ter 'ave one in 'ere." Lucy heaved herself to her feet and followed Eliza out of the sickroom. "What's up wiv 'im anyway?" she asked. Eliza explained that Phillip did not have long to live, that the cancer eating his bones was advanced; time was running out for the elderly gentleman.
"Poor sod!" responded Lucy, "I 'ope 'e'll 'ave long enough to sort the boy out."

***

Some considerable time later, and after several more 'fag' breaks, Lucy finished explaining her story. She told of how she had placed the newspaper announcements in the hope that Phillip might see them and respond. By enquiring of the editorial team as to who had placed them he had allowed Lucy, via his telephone number, to locate him in Minchington. In such a small village it didn't take much effort to find out where he lived and while he had been pondering over the coincidence of names, she was already on her way to see him and spill her enormous can of worms. It was a surprisingly clever ruse and he couldn't help but be impressed with her ingenuity; perhaps there had been something more than lust in their past union.

"My poor Cathy can't look after 'im no more. She can't even look after 'erself. She won't come out of that 'ome again now. She's lost 'er mind yer see. An' I'm too old to take the boy in, an' anyways I don' 'ave much dosh, so 'e needs your 'elp. After all 'e is yours too."

She left only after he had promised to do what he could to help her grandson; his grandson. He really had no idea as to quite how that help was to manifest itself but at least she knew roughly whereabouts the boy was living and although she had no definite address, she knew how to contact Sir Randolph's School where he had been a pupil at one time. She left the details with Eliza. "Well, she seems like a nice lady, I feel I can trust 'er," thought the old woman as she made her way haltingly down the lane towards the village and the bus stop, "She'll see the boy's alright."

Chapter Twenty-Three

"I really don't think you should go!" Timothy was outraged at the thought of his grandmother leaving to go gallivanting across the country on a whim. Of course she had not enlightened him as to the real reason for her trip. Instead she had led him to believe, without being specific, that she wished to pay a visit to an old friend who was sick and likely to die. It was the truth; apart from the 'friend'. Was he a friend? How could she be friends with the man who had treated her sister so damnably?

"You're sick yourself Grandmother," he railed and then added, "I'm coming with you." The declaration was met with a refusal, "No Timothy, I'm afraid you can't, not this time. Elsa will take care of me and I will be back in no time at all. Don't upset yourself, you know what might happen if you become over stressed."

Timothy was further incensed by this remark. It was almost taboo to mention his 'problem' in his hearing. He was determined to ignore any suggestion that he was anything but perfect in every way and as he grew into adulthood, those he loved understood that he dealt with his malady by accepting it as part of normality. Therefore, any specific references to stress or tension and their possible or even probably consequences were forbidden. He slammed out of the room and thundered up the stairs to his room calling back, "Don't blame me if it all goes wrong then!" Eleanor smiled ruefully to herself and continued to make preparations for her visit. She wasn't at all sure what to expect but she knew that Elsa would look after her and all would become clear in due course.

***

He really couldn't explain why he felt so strongly. It was just an overwhelming feeling of dread. Something terribly wrong and something was about to change, perhaps irrevocably. He buried his head in Snowball's fur and took comfort from the soft pink tongue that washed his face. The aging dog spent most of his days curled asleep on Timothy's bed. A truce was called between him and Peanut who similarly slept on the blanket box placed beneath the window and next to a radiator. Thomas had long since moved into the spare room across the hall, but Peanut preferred the sunny side of the house and only ventured into his master's room at night.

After a while, and sighing deeply, Timothy scrambled off the bed, smoothed the counterpane and made his way downstairs to apologise for his outspokenness. Instead of his grandmother, he found Elsa folding up the last of Eleanor's discarded garments and putting them carefully away in the chest of drawers. She took one look at his drawn face and invited him to come in, sit down and chat.

"I don't know what the matter is with me at the moment," he began, "my head's all over the place and I just keep feeling so angry with everything and everyone. It's like I can't control anything anymore. Especially not myself! I didn't mean to be rude to Grandmother; it just came out all wrong."

Elsa put the last of the clothes away and came to stand behind his chair. Massaging his tense shoulders, she soothed and reassured him; "It's all quite normal for someone of your age..." she began...

"Don't patronise me!" he retorted angrily and shrugged his shoulders out from under her hands; "You and I both know that there is something very un-normal about my life." She was surprised to hear him say it aloud. Of course she had known since coming here, and indeed the whole reason for her being at Willow Lodge, that his life path would be a bumpy road but she hadn't expected him to acknowledge this truth; not so soon. He was obviously far more astute than she had realised. She sat down carefully on the edge of Eleanor's bed and took his hands into her own. "Try to understand that I only want to help you." She looked into his eyes and was moved by the troubled soul that she saw there. "I think maybe it's time..." she murmured quietly.

"For what?" he questioned, still with an air of irritation.

"For me to fulfil a promise," she responded, "I must make some arrangements first but bear with me and I will do my best to help you understand what is happening to you and why life sometimes seems to be so difficult. I know that you are aware of things that other people don't always see or appreciate and perhaps now you can no longer pretend that it is not so. There is a purpose behind it all and it's time you knew more about why things happen as they do. Please forbear. Try to not take out your anguish on others, especially those who love you, and I will do what I can as soon as I am able to make the necessary arrangements. Be patient my boy." A long silence ensued as the two gazed deeply into each other's soul until Timothy sniffed mightily and smiled a watery smile at this woman who had been a central part of his life for as long as he could remember. Mother figure, guardian, friend, nurse and mentor, she meant the world to him and he leaned forward and kissed her lightly on her cheek. "Thanks," he muttered gruffly before rising clumsily to his feet and leaving the room; his gangling half-grown limbs not always obeying his subconscious commands as he stumbled through the doorway and took himself out into the garden. He disappeared through the hanging branches of the old willow tree and made his way to his favourite spot by the little muddy stream. There he could find peace and solitude and try to make sense of all the inequities that tainted his otherwise happy existence.

***

In due course, Elsa and Eleanor drew up outside the big old house in Minchington. The journey had been uneventful and less arduous than Eleanor had feared. They had stopped at a roadside café and partaken of coffee and tea cakes about thirty minutes before the appointed hour of arrival. Elsa, a very capable driver, was wonderful at inconsequential chat and had managed to distract Eleanor from her concerns as to the purpose of this visit. She was curious about her late sister's former husband but her curiosity was tinged with distaste; she wouldn't go as far as dislike since she had never met the man, but he had certainly treated Jen with disdain and cruelty. And now they had arrived and were soon mounting the few steps to the big old oak front door which was opened before they had even raised the knocker to announce their presence.

"Welcome!" smiled Eliza as she ushered them into the hallway. She offered them tea, which they politely refused, and took their outer garments, placing them carefully on a strategically placed chair. "Phillip is just waking from his afternoon nap. Would you wait in here," she indicated a small parlour to the right of the front door, "or would you prefer to stretch your legs in the garden?" Eleanor chose to wait inside but Elsa elected to re-don her jacket and strolled outside saying, "I don't think you need me to stay with you when you meet Phillip and I'd like to walk a bit before we set off for home. Is that alright with you?"

Having received Eleanor's blessing, Elsa slipped out of the room as Eliza crossed the hallway to rouse Phillip and prepare him for his visitor.

The meeting was brief. Phillip's condition was deteriorating rapidly and conversation was limited to short exchanges and long pauses during which he closed his eyes and to all intents and purposes appeared to be asleep. It was during one of these pauses that Eleanor glanced out of the big bay window, appreciating its panoramic view of the neatly kept grounds. She saw Elsa walking slowly, admiring the budding snowdrops and crocuses and enjoying the weak spring sunshine. As she watched, Eleanor saw another figure hurrying across the lawn toward Elsa. They greeted each other warmly and linked arms as, heads bowed close; they continued on their way and soon began to disappear from Eleanor's view. She stepped forward into the bay to see more clearly whence they went, and it seemed to her that the two figures merged into one and she could no longer distinguish one from the other. For a short while, she pondered this phenomenon but the wisdom of her years and her experience of strange occurrences throughout her life, allowed her to set her thoughts aside and remain focused on the enormity of what Phillip was asking of her.

***

There was no need for words between Elsa and Eliza. Each knew the other and each knew their individual role. They linked arms as they walked and their communication was silent as their hearts beat as one and their limbs blended into one gait. As they reached the gate into the meadow beyond the garden, Old Bess stepped forward and held her arms wide. She folded the girls into her ample bosom and kissed their cheek. "I am well pleased with you," she smiled and took their hand. "A little longer now and all will be done," she reassured. For a moment she looked into their eyes and then she nodded, "Bring him soon; it is time." She embraced the girl again and then she was gone. The single slight figure of Elsa resumed her slow perambulation back across the garden.

***

A light tap on the door heralded the reappearance of Eliza, carrying a tray laden with tea for Eleanor and various medicinal paraphernalia for Phillip. For a brief moment Eleanor considered the impossibility of what she had just witnessed however, she once again dismissed her thoughts as irrelevant and smiled at Eliza who was both familiar and yet a stranger. Once she had administered the requisite medicine to her patient, Eliza excused herself and made to leave the room but Phillip raised his hand and croakily asked that she stay a while; he wanted her to witness his request.

***

For a long time the homeward journey was without conversation. Both Elsa and Eleanor were deep in thought. Eleanor was also weary, the travel and the emotional nature of the visit had taken its toll. She leaned back in the comfortable seat and let her thoughts wash over her. Had she made the right decision? Of course, he was disappointed

116

but she hadn't left him entirely unsatisfied. She had found him pitiable; she didn't hate him and any anger that she may have felt on her sister's behalf had dissipated the moment she realised how he suffered. Karma? Perhaps; it has a way of balancing things out. She smiled weakly to herself, realising that she felt nothing at all for this old man except gratitude. Without him, she may never have known her niece-come-daughter, Tam who had meant the world to her and who had given her a reason to live.

"So will you do it?" Eleanor was startled by Elsa's sudden question. Not only because she had broken into the silence of Eleanor's reverie but also because she had not mentioned Phillip's request. How could Elsa know what was asked? Realising that she had shaken the older woman's thoughts, Elsa pulled in to a lay-by and stopped the engine. "I'm sorry!" she opined, "I didn't mean to upset you."

"No, it's fine, but… how did you…" Eleanor broke off and peered into Elsa's face. Elsa smiled, "I know everything!" she laughed, making light of the situation.

"Of course you do," Eleanor, more serious now, replied. "Then if you know everything, you will know what my answer is." For a few moments, they were silent until, without further comment, Elsa restarted the car and the rest of the journey home was made in companionable silence and occasional superficial chit chat to pass the time.

Chapter Twenty-Four

The legal paperwork and solicitors' letters were reminiscent of all those years ago when Tam and Simon had adopted Shane and Carrie. It all took time; time that was in short supply for Phillip. Several times Simon drove to Minchington in order to speed up the process. Avoiding delays in the postal service was essential and Phillip had never subscribed to email; had never even possessed a computer or the internet. Lucy had been a little more difficult to trace but the Psychiatric hospital that was home to Cathy provided the necessary details and eventually, in the shortest time possible, all was in order and Thomas was formally adopted by Rosa and Simon. Eleanor had not felt able to take on the responsibility by herself but when she explained the situation to Simon, he had offered without any hesitation to provide a life-long home for the boy who had already become such an integral part of the family. Carrie was delighted and kept referring to Thomas as her "Ickle Bruvver!" although, truth to tell, he was a lot larger than she. Shane slapped Thomas heartily on the back and welcomed him as his "Bro'," Snowball yapped excitedly and an impromptu party ensued.

It was during this happy time that the phone rang. Timothy took the call and all fell silent when he re-entered the room with a sombre look on his face. "Uncle Phillip is dead," he announced bluntly.

**

Head bowed and shoulders slumped, Heather knelt beside the small headstone that leant at a slightly crazy angle against the Oak trunk that grew from behind the retaining wall of the grave. Now she was entirely alone. The small number of guests had gone soon after the food was finished, the wine drunk and the insincere condolences uttered. Eliza had been a marvel. She had organised everything, taken responsibility for tidying the house and putting it ready to sell. Of course she couldn't deal with the legal side of things; probate, the

Will, the Trust funds, but she had done her best to make it as easy as possible for Heather and she was grateful. Kate's grave was in a sorry state and she determined to come back soon and restore it to its former glory whilst also tending to the very new grave at its side. Would Kate be pleased to see Phillip? Would Kate still be there? Heather sighed; she wasn't as alone as she had been, she had her dogs and her cats and the occasional visit from Bertie, who loved her when he hadn't got anything better to do. Above all she had her crafts which she enjoyed and which kept her occupied so that she didn't dwell on her aloneness. With Phillip gone, there would perhaps eventually be a little more money; from the sale of the big house, and perhaps, as she had often dreamt, she could open a little shop. "Hmmm," she mused, "'Kate's parlour'. I'd better get a move on with it because I'm certainly not getting any younger!"

***

Eleanor felt sorry that she hadn't attended the funeral. She had sent some flowers and a message of sympathy to Heather. She thought that perhaps she should have taken Thomas to his grandfather's funeral... She felt guilty...

"Now, now, no wallowing in self-pity!" Elsa's bright voice broke into her mournful reverie, "I need to take Timothy away for a little while and just want to be sure that you can manage without me?" Without waiting for an answer, she continued, "You mustn't berate yourself. He didn't really know you, or you him."

"I know, I know, but Heather..."

"Heather will be fine. She is one of the most resilient people I have ever met. I should imagine she is already planning how she will spend her inheritance! I don't mean to suggest that she is unfeeling, but she certainly knows how to keep her spirits up and to be positive about things. We could all take a lesson from her!"

The two women smiled at each other in a bond of mutual understanding, "Just give me time and I'll be fine," smiled Eleanor.

***

The wind blew no less and the path grew even steeper than the first time she had come here. How long ago? She knew not. She had been coming here for as long as she could remember and the welcome was always the same. Cats, cakes, coffee and the all-encompassing embrace from Old Bess.

"Is he with you?" she asked as she pushed Elsa away from her. Hands on her shoulders and looking at her from arms' length, she remarked, "You look exhausted child! Come and sit down."

"He wanted to walk on the beach," Elsa replied, "and anyway I wanted to speak with you alone. So it sort of worked as things always seem to around here." She smiled wryly. Old Bess bustled round her small, untidy kitchen, and produced a pot of tea and a plate of hot buttered crumpets. "How is he?" she asked.

A short while later a loud thump on the door heralded Timothy's arrival. Out of breath, his unkempt locks windswept and wild, his cheeks rosy and with the soft down of an adolescent face, he came into the room bringing with him the aroma of fresh air, salt and youth. He was positively glowing.

Once he had sated his appetite and was comfortably ensconced in a big old armchair, Old Bess began...

"Elsa tells me that you have questioned your condition and your purpose. No don't answer, listen. You must understand that we all have a purpose in life on earth and many, no, most, people never know what that purpose is. That is always assuming that they have actually stopped to consider the reasons for their being. We believe we know why we are born; to live, love, laugh and to make money and leave our mark on earth and yes, of course that is a part of it all. I would add to procreate and to learn too and certainly to experience. Moreover, for some people there are greater purposes. Most believe we are born, we live, we die but in reality there is much more than that. Between dying and being re-born there is another place; perhaps a sort of limbo or holding bay. Sometimes we are held in limbo for a long time, usually because of some unfinished business either on one side or the other." Timothy's eyes began to close. Not because he was disinterested in what Old Bess was telling him but because of a combination of fresh air and good food and the singsong soporific tone of her voice. Gradually he was lulled into a dreamlike state that was neither asleep nor awake.

At first he had wondered why Elsa had brought him to this place. He had assumed it was a day out at the beach, but then why was Thomas not included in the invitation? As they neared Old Bess's cottage, he realised that he knew this place; that he had been here before. He recognised the old lady, although he could not have said how he knew her. He simply knew that she belonged to him and to everyone who needed her. As he relaxed into the lullaby of her voice, his mind swirled with thoughts, figures and half-remembered memories.

'She stepped lightly across the grass and sat beside him, knowing that he would not fear her presence. He looked directly at her and murmured, "About time too! Do you know how long I have waited for you?" Tam looked surprised; this wasn't the sort of greeting she expected. But then again, she wasn't sure what sort of salutation she had anticipated. He grinned at her and held out his hand. There in his palm lay the pebble that had passed from her to Carrie and from Carrie to him. "Take it," he said, "I have no need of it now but you must return it to whence it came. For everything must come full circle, just as ripples move in circles, and your circle is complete."

It did not occur to her to wonder how he knew these things any more than she had questioned her own knowledge of inexplicable ideas and strange phenomena.

"Take it," he repeated insistently.

Timothy had grown quickly into the young man beside her. It seemed only such a short while since she had held the newborn infant in her arms, and yet here he was, already understanding so much more than she had in her time. His journey would also be hard at times. However, he had a sense of humour and sufficient strength of character to overcome any obstacle in his path and he had the foundation of a loving, moral family to support and guide him. Only Tam knew just how hard it could be and yet she would not have changed any part of her time here in the physical world; not even the inexplicable spiritual experiences that had coloured her life.

She did not speak. She took him in her arms and held him close. "Go carefully, be strong and trust that you will be guided." He heard her silent message and embraced her wholly as he closed his eyes and smiled; a wide grin that crinkled his young eyes even while shuttered, and produced two delightfully charming dimples, one in either cheek.'

Into his hand, she pressed something small and hard, "Not yet Timothy, not yet," she whispered.

***

The beatific smile on his face reassured Elsa that he had understood what Old Bess was showing him. The old lady leant forward and took his hand. Stroking the soft skin, she explained how his malady was key to his purpose. She asked him to accept and not to fight. That no harm would come to him and that, in time, he would be given a difficult choice to make. In response he simply nodded as he held out his hand to her, his opened palm revealing the small round golden pebble... and then he slept.

Chapter Twenty-Five

She had been there every morning for the last two weeks and still he had not plucked up the courage to speak to her! Her glorious, unkempt, red curls framed her fresh, young face on either cheek of which dimples insisted on puckering the light dusting of freckles that dotted her otherwise clear complexion. He, late as always, came hurtling round the last bend before the bus stop, rucksack straps flapping and coat tails flying behind him, and skidded to a halt a few yards short of the bench on which she perched. It was not like him to be lost for words but he found himself silenced by her presence and he shifted his feet awkwardly and ineffectively straightened his tie while he waited for Thomas who lumbered clumsily behind him. There followed a short pause which was soon filled by the arrival of the bus and the two boys stood back politely waiting for her to board first.

"Go on," nudged Thomas, "speak to her! You know you want to!" Instead Timothy punched his friend roughly and told him to shut up; he'd talk to her when he was ready.

"You'll never be ready," grumbled Thomas, rubbing his shoulder, "and if you don't do it soon, I will. Then you won't stand a chance!" He grinned at Timothy, knowing as they both did that he was by far the more charismatic of the two. Thus it was, in feigned annoyance, they continued to playfully punch and cuff each other for a few minutes more until laughing softly together, they settled into their seats for the twenty minute journey to college.

***

At eighteen Timothy was a good looking and charming young man who enjoyed life to the full. He was tall and slender and had retained his unruly blonde hair and bright blue eyes. Many girls had set their sights on gaining his attention but he was not particularly interested in any of them besides he was wary of his 'condition' knowing that it could be frightening to witness and had already chased a few potential friends away. Nevertheless, acquaintances came easily and he was content to have an eclectic crew of casual buddies who shared his various interests but without whom he was equally happy. He had always enjoyed his own company and did not need people around him to stimulate or entertain. In truth he preferred being alone.

Thomas was the exception to this state of affairs but Thomas never intruded upon Timothy's seclusion, he instinctively knew that it was important to Timothy to have time to himself and so he would watch from a distance. He kept a check on Timothy's whereabouts without imposing restriction and was never judgemental; his role was to observe and, if possible, to warn when an episode was imminent. He had developed an unerring sense of knowing when Timothy was in danger of having a fit and Timothy trusted him completely. Thus the bond that was formed when they were young had strengthened as the years passed. No longer confined to Sir Randolph's, Thomas had seamlessly slotted into his now formalised role at Willow Lodge. His own continuing health problems prevented him from being as active as his best friend and adoptive brother but he enrolled himself on a course in IT engineering at the local college and whenever his timetable matched Timothy's they travelled together. His growing skills were invaluable to Simon, who struggled to grasp the finer points of modern technology.

**

Having failed to meet the required grades for entry to veterinary college whilst still at school, Timothy's determination to follow his chosen, ambitious career had led him to enrol to retake his exams at college. However, much to Rosa and Simon's consternation, and despite his own seeming lack of concern, Timothy's petit mal was developing into something more serious and the frequency of episodes increasing. They had always hoped that adulthood would bring relief, that he would grow out of the problem but their hopes were fading and so they began the arduous process of working their

124

way through a minefield of medical opinion in order to find a solution.

Nonetheless, Timothy was determined to live life to the full and paid little heed to the obstacles that threatened to prevent him. However, the most recent of these had resulted in an uncharacteristic fit of pique when it became abundantly clear that he would not be granted a provisional driving licence. Ranting and railing about the injustices of the world and everyone in it, he marched out of the house and disappeared for several hours. Everyone, after their initial astonishment, grew more and more concerned as he failed to reappear and eventually Elsa, with the ancient Snowball in tow, set off to look for him.

***

He knew it was going to happen; he always knew when it was going to happen, but it was part of his refusal to acknowledge its effect on his life that he chose to ignore the warnings. Oh they had told him often enough that it was dangerous to fail to react; he could fall and bang his head, he could fall into water and drown, he could fall under a fast moving vehicle, he could fall…

"I know!" he muttered fiercely to himself, "I know!" he shouted to the sky, "I bloody well know!" and at that precise moment the front wheel of his bicycle hit a small rock and buckled, throwing him unceremoniously, upside down, into a muddy ditch.

Chapter Twenty-Six

The day dragged interminably. Rain drizzled dismally down the windowpanes and the damp seemed to seep into the very structure of the ancient building. Even the old dog seemed restless. Heaving himself to his feet, he padded around the room and dropping down onto the hearth rug with a heartfelt sigh, raised his baleful eyes to where she sat and willed her to notice his discontent.

She worked single-mindedly. The fabric twisting and turning in her hands as the needle darted in and out, the yarn weaving an intricate pattern. Her fingers flew and the garment took shape, a rich tapestry of colours spilling across her lap and flowing onto the sofa beside her. It had to be done today! She had to have it finished before nightfall...

Tomorrow! It seemed impossible that this day had arrived at last. Surely it was only a few short months ago that Tod had come to her with his exciting if somewhat disconcerting news. Anna paused, needle held high mid stitch, and glanced at the photograph which took pride of place on the mantelpiece. Smiling back at her were the happy faces of her son and his fiancée. She was such a pretty woman although there was a guarded sadness behind her eyes. The girl never spoke of her past and Anna understood that there were things too painful to take out and re-examine; some things are best kept locked away in our hearts. Nevertheless, she couldn't help but be inquisitive about this woman who was taking away her son. Bohemian in style and with a powerful love of bright colours and glitzy glamour, she had requested that Anna make the extraordinary wedding dress. Laid over the back of a dining chair was the coat of many colours she had already completed for Tod and now she put the finishing touches to the fantastic gown in readiness for tomorrow.

Tomorrow. A sigh wracked Anna's slight body and she unthinkingly put her hand down to receive a comforting lick from Billy's ever ready tongue. If only she could rid herself of this overriding sense of foreboding. Wild in style and wild by nature, Sandra was so insular that Anna felt she knew precious little about the girl. Of course she knew that she was a nurse; at least they had that in common, and yet there was so much more that she would like to know. Where and who were her parents? Did she have any family; relations or even friends? The wedding party was to be extremely small, just a few of Tod's family, friends, herself and Tomo and no one to give the bride away? It all seemed so mysterious and strange in spite of Sandra's reassurance that she was happy for it to be so.

Anna thought back to her own extravagant wedding. Too extravagant really! Hundreds, or so it seemed, of guests; many in military uniform, enough food to feed the entire army and a full orchestra to dance to. Not to mention the month long honeymoon in Barbados, all paid for by Harold Stanton, her late enigmatic father-in-law who seemed to be trying to compensate for his earlier failings as a father. She sighed again as a wistful smile twitched the corners of her mouth. Little did they know then that she would have been just as happy to have a smaller civil wedding; just her and Tomo… she paused in her reminiscing; maybe the girl was not so strange after all? Though not for the world would she have missed the pride in her father's eyes as he walked her down the aisle and by placing her hand in Tomo's, gave her away to the man she loved.

***

A gentle knock at the door heralded the arrival of an unexpected guest. Billy, tail wagging wildly, woofed a warning and Anna laid aside the garment, careful to gather its folds to prevent the yards of fabric from dragging on the floor.

She did not recognise the bedraggled young man who stood smiling on her doorstep. "I seem to have come unstuck!" he cheerfully announced and a quick glance up and down his lanky body confirmed his muddy and dishevelled state. "I'm sorry to disturb you on such a night as this," continued the stranger, "but I was coming to see you anyway and then I fell." Without stopping to consider the implication of his words, Anna ushered him into the hall and carefully slipped his sodden coat from his shoulders. As she helped him to wipe the mire from his face, she realised that he was far younger than she had first thought; no more than a boy. What was he doing out here on a night like this and why would he have been coming to visit her? She did not know him.

Before long he was cleaned and, wearing one of Tomo's nightgowns, sipped hot cocoa while his damp clothes were spread to dry on radiators and the fire guard. The completed wedding gown had been carefully folded away in readiness for the morrow. Anna had not wanted to disturb Tomo; he was sleeping upstairs and she knew that the following day was going to take its toll on her husband; not only physically but a drain on his emotional strength also. His resistance was already lowered by his disability, the ongoing aftermath of his long stay in hospital and even longer period of convalescence and rehabilitation. Age too was leaving its mark; its cruel attacks doubly harsh on his already battered body. Nevertheless, his prosthetic limb was remarkable and few people, meeting him for the first time, even realised that he wore one.

Timothy interrupted her thoughts by gently touching her arm as he leant forward to speak. "Thank you," he said. She smiled and began to form a response but before she could utter the words he pressed a finger to her lips and said, "Hush. I know that you want to ask questions but please just listen; I don't have much time." Puzzled she complied with his request and took his chilled hand and held it in her warm ones whilst gently caressing the fine young skin.

"I came to tell you not to worry; to reassure you that things are working out just as they should." How did he know of her concerns? Who was this young man? Again, he quieted her tumbling mind, "It doesn't matter who I am or where I come from but it matters that you understand that there are some things we cannot control." He paused and gazed deeply into her eyes, searching her soul with his brilliant blue orbs, "Do you remember how you met Tomo?" he asked. Anna nodded.

She had been a physiotherapist at the convalescence home where Tomo had spent many months learning to walk again and dealing with the mental scars his traumatic experience had caused. She had known that Tomo was 'the one' the first time she saw him. How do we know such things? Yet know it she had and as time passed and Tomo grew in confidence and strength, love had grown and deepened between them until, with Harold Stanton's blessing, they were married in extravagant style in the Military Chapel; the same Chapel in which, tomorrow, their son Tod would be wed. The same Chapel that provided the focal point of the converted barracks in which they still lived in Harold's old quarters.

"I understand your concerns for your son but you must know that he loves Sandra as you have loved Tomo. I know that they are meant to be together. Don't ask me how I know but please accept what I tell you. Sandra is a good woman and she will be loyal, faithful and will care for Tod. She will provide you all with great joy and comfort. Do not question her enigmatic nature; sometimes there are things that are too personal to share and so we keep them to ourselves. She is protecting you all from her pain. Respect her right to her silence. Remember her joy in colour and music – these are the things that make her who she is."

The boy ran his finger lightly over her face and across her eyelids. Her eyes closed involuntarily and she kept them so for a few seconds. When she opened them he was gone. Placed neatly on the chair were Tomo's nightgown and the empty mug. Gone too were the drying clothes. Had she dreamt it all? Was her mind playing tricks on her now? She glanced around the room looking for signs of his recent presence but there were none. It was only when she turned back to the fireplace to tidy away the remaining sewing paraphernalia that the exquisite perfume assailed her nostrils and made her look up to the mantelpiece. There, in front of the framed engagement picture of Tod and Sandra, in all its pearly white iridescent perfection and nestling in its heart a solitary diamond dewdrop, lay a perfectly formed Rose.

Chapter Twenty-Seven

Sirens split the silence of the street. Timothy was oblivious to the stir that he had caused. Sunk into the profound somnolence that always followed an attack, he neither heard nor saw Snowball whose excited yapping alerted Elsa to the whereabouts of her charge. Following her intuition and aided and abetted by the faithful dog, she had traced his path to the muddy ditch in which he now lay. Although it was obvious to her that he had suffered a fit; which state of affairs did not concern her unduly, it was also apparent that there was something wrong with his left arm which lay at a peculiar angle, partially trapped by the somewhat mangled bicycle. Reluctant to move him during the aftermath of his attack, since doing so could sometimes trigger a repeat performance, she took off her coat and laid it over his bedraggled body, taking care to not disturb his damaged arm. She used her mobile phone to call for an ambulance and then pressed her warm body as close to his as she could get; sharing her warmth in the damp and confined space in the ditch. Snowball tucked himself in beside Timothy's head, resting his own possessively across the prostrate form.

Although she knew all that Old Bess had taught her, and although she knew that hers was to watch and protect as best she could, she desperately wished that she could take away this awful malady from the golden boy. Ever since she had taken him to Old Bess, he had renewed his determination to live a full and normal life. He never mentioned the visit and neither did she although she detected a new depth to his character and a greater gentleness and maturity in his manner. He brought so much joy to his parents and to Eleanor and Carrie and he seemed to spread light and peace wherever he went. Why then did he have to suffer? She closed her tear laden eyes as she pondered on the seeming injustice of it all…

"He will not suffer although it may seem that way." Old Bess leant forward speaking earnestly and emphasising

130

her words with the tap of a forefinger on Elsa's knee. "It is necessary in order to find a way for him to complete his tasks. Your duty is not to prevent these things from happening but to keep him safe when they do. You will be helped and guided in this responsibility; you are never alone. If you need support for yourself, just ask and it will be given to you."

The flashing of the blue lights penetrated her closed eyelids and the sirens wailed a greeting as the ambulance drew to a standstill beside the strange and by now very muddy group.

"Now, now, which is the casualty?" chuckled the burly paramedic as he stepped down from the cab with far greater agility than his size suggested. Elsa scrambled carefully to her feet revealing the dishevelled form sleeping peacefully beneath the bicycle. "Ah! Now I see..." as he realised the true situation. "Come away, mutt," he commanded and gently removed Snowball from his guard. Snowball struggled briefly but allowed himself to be put into Elsa's arms; all the time keeping his eyes firmly fixed on his master. Stepping lightly from the far side of the vehicle, another medic carried a large red blanket and other rescue equipment; her diminutive but chubby form belied her strength as she helped lift the distorted bike in order to more easily assess the situation. She paused briefly as she passed Elsa and looked closely at her to check that she was unhurt. Elsa gasped as she recognised the twinkling eyes and wisps of greying hair that escaped from the waterproof hood of a high visibility jacket. The briefest of flickers of an eyelid and a slight nod of the head confirmed her surprised suspicion as...

"Betty!" called her partner, "We're going to need that back slab! Can you get it for me please?"

***

It hadn't been long before Timothy was home, sporting a bright white plaster cast and cheerfully laughing at his own clumsiness whilst bemoaning the destruction of his rather expensive road bike.

"If that is what you do with a bicycle, I think it's a good job they won't give you a driving licence!" Simon hid his worries with a jocular remark.

"Oh come on Dad," retorted Timothy, "I'd have been much safer on four wheels. They don't tip you off quite so unceremoniously! Although I suppose it would have cost a great deal more to get a car out of the ditch!" Timothy's irrepressible good humour had returned and the only minor marring of his mood was his impatience to get back onto a rugby pitch.

Eleanor shook her head and glanced at Rosa. The two women shared a brief moment of mutual understanding before Eleanor's rich roll of laughter rang out more strongly than her aging frame suggested. "That boy will be the death of me!" she exclaimed.

Chapter Twenty-Eight

One more glance in the long mirror showed her a tall, slim woman in her mid-fifties. Dressed in a classic, French blue gown and jacket, wearing low heeled white court shoes and carrying a matching clutch bag, she was the epitome of elegance. Not high fashion, just understated class and timeless style. With her once dark hair, now streaked with silver, swept up into a chignon and held in place by diamante pins and with a small fascinator perched securely on top, she glided down the broad oak staircase to where Tomo stood waiting for her.

"Time to go," he announced and held out his crooked arm for hers to slip through. He kissed her lightly on her cheek, "You look absolutely stunning my darling," he breathed into her hair.

A few minutes later, they arrived at the chapel having crossed the parade ground slowly and carefully avoiding the growing number of cracks and potholes. It was a glorious early summer morning with wall to wall sunshine in a dazzlingly blue sky. Together they entered the small chapel and made their way to the reserved pew on the right hand side as is traditional for the parents of the groom. Tod turned to greet them; no sign of nerves and a wide grin indicated his excitement and joy at the occasion. Anna proffered her cheek for a kiss from her son and Tomo clasped his hand and pulled him to his chest as they clapped each other on the shoulder in a wordless man-hug. After a few seconds during which they both struggled to control the threatening overflow of emotions, the two men broke apart and, "Well son," began the elder, "this is it! Are you ready?" A brief nod reassured him as he settled into his somewhat uncomfortable seat. The small organ began to play and as the gentle strains of 'Jesu' Joy of Man's Desiring filled the vaulted spaces, Tomo's mind drifted back to the last time he had sat in this place...

***

The sulphurous smell of gun smoke suffused his senses, eyes tightly closed to keep out the stinging acrid fumes, his ears deafened by the continuous crash and thunder of the tanks; he ran. He had never run so fast in all his life, it seemed as though he flew, his feet barely touching the sucking muddy ground. He knew he was screaming but his ears heard nothing, he knew he was crying but his tears could not fall from his unseeing eyes. He fell. Landing face down in the mud, excruciating pain; running no longer; he groaned as his maimed body thrashed under the covers, his face buried in the pillow and sheets. A familiar voice, a cool dry hand stroking his forehead, unheard words soothing him, reassuring him, "It's over son, it's all over, I'm here, you're safe…" again and again the same phrases until at last he began to relax the rigour that had wracked him in paroxysms of fear. For a few minutes longer he kept his eyes shut. His breathing slowed and his limbs eased their rigidity.

His father watched and wished he could wipe away the memories that haunted his sleep. The body heals but the mind hides its pain until the subconscious rules the night. Sergeant Stanton could only imagine the awfulness of his son's experience. There were many, many times when he had thanked his lucky stars that he had not been called to serve on the front line, however, now he would give anything and everything to have been in his son's place on that fateful and terrible day. He brushed away yet another tear and sniffing back the threatening tide of emotion, breathed deeply and left his son's bedside to fetch a comforting, cure-all, cup of tea.

Tomo awoke, blinked in the bright morning sunlight that spilled over the windowsill, and glanced across the room at the crumpled pillow pressed into the old brown leather armchair. He smiled wryly to himself in the knowledge that his father had spent yet another night watching him.

It had been a few months earlier, whilst he was still hospitalised in a rehabilitation ward, that his father had come to him. Tomo had awoken one morning to find a pretty nurse tapping him gently on the

134

shoulder, "There's someone here to see you," she announced, "he's been waiting for some time but he said I wasn't to disturb you. May I send him in now or would you like to freshen up first?" Tomo had had very few visitors, mainly because he shunned anyone who might have come, but also because he did not want empty pity or sympathetic words declaring that they 'know how you feel!' How could they possibly know unless the same loss had happened to them? At first even his parents had been held at bay.

Soon after the extraordinary events on the evening of Jay's visitation he had accepted a visitor. His heart broke when he saw the grief etched on his mother's face; one son maimed for life and the other dead. Both had been sacrificed to the wild wantonness of war, whose dangerous depravity had destroyed the unfulfilled futures of so many. She could barely contain her tears but held him close, avoided asking about his leg, and promised to tell Harold to come soon. Tomo knew that she would not come again. It was too much to ask, too much pain to bear, and so the tables were turned and his mother became the absentee parent while his father willingly took on the task of supporting and encouraging his son to live as full a life as possible.

At first he visited weekly and each time he came he brought a single white rosebud. Tomo did not need to ask him why; the words remained unspoken between them but both knew that something extraordinary had occurred and both realised and recognised the symbolism of the solitary bloom.

Chapter Twenty-Nine

No one had asked whether it should happen that way, it just did and no one objected; it was simply taken for granted that Harold would care for his son until such time as the son would need to care for the father. Before long Tomo had been transferred to a physiotherapy unit closer to home and later, when various alterations had been made, to the old barracks where his father still resided. Their reconciliation was complete.

In due course the inevitable time came when the aging Harold could no longer manage to run the house by himself. His arthritic bones called for a walking frame and his increasing forgetfulness made for awkward situations. Anna, in her capacity as a physiotherapist, had by now become a regular visitor to the house, and on recognising that they both needed more help than either could give the other, she volunteered to take on the duties of keeping house and of assisting where necessary. Oblivious to the budding romance between his son and the pretty young nurse, Harold was only too pleased to accept her into his home. He was not unduly dismayed; indeed he was really rather pleased when, in the space of a few short months, Anna and Tomo were husband and wife; married in the old chapel, with as much pomp and circumstance as he could muster and happily ensconced in the big old house that was more than spacious enough for all three.

Harold felt that his life was complete. He often regretted his earlier distance from his family, especially from his children when they were young, and told himself that he did not deserve to have such happiness at this time of his life. Upon the arrival of little Tod, his joy knew no bounds and for a short time Tomo saw glimpses of the father he'd never had. Far from being sad and resentful, he revelled in his father's happiness. Together they had conquered pride, changed courses and found a mutual interest in improving their individual situation. One had found the strength to walk on into a brighter future and the other a salve with which to sooth his injured soul.

There was only one small cloud which threatened their equilibrium from time to time and that was the absence of Jay. At times Tomo thought on his brother; where would he have been had he lived? What sort of a life would he have made for himself? Would he have found a similar peace to that which prevailed in this place? Often he would catch a distant sadness in his father's eyes and yet it was a sorrow that they shared and even that sharing drew them closer. Nevertheless, as time took its toll on Harold's physical form; dementia clouded his mind and gradually memories, together with sight and sound, were lost. His joie de vivre gently faded away until, one morning a peaceful shadow of his former self failed to awake. At the age of eighty-one, Harold Stanton died.

***

The last time Tomo had sat in this same place had been for Harold's funeral service and Tomo smiled to himself. Of course it had been a sad occasion but it could have been an empty and far less significant a passing had he not had those final years, both to get to know his father and to prove himself worthy as his son.

Entering Harold's room several days prior to the service, in order to collect his father's military uniform in which he was to be interred; highlighted by a soft shaft of sunlight from the unshuttered window, the envelope had caught his eye. Tomo had read his father's final words again and again over the years and still they continued, without fail, to remind him that it really is never too late to make amends.

Dear Tomo, my son of whom I am so very proud.

I do not know how to express all that I would like you to know and so I hope you will forgive an old man for wrapping my message in a story that I once heard a long time ago. I was reminded of it a short while ago when I overheard you remark to Anna that you did not have time to meet up with your old army friends.

Make time my boy! All too soon your time will be gone, your friends will be gone and your opportunities will be gone. I so very nearly missed my chance to make amends with you – I do not want you to do the same.

For many years I buried myself in busyness; I avoided addressing the issues that need resolving, I made myself important when, truth to tell, in the wider scheme of things, I was extremely unimportant. A two bit Sergeant in a two bit army pushing worthless pieces of paper around an over polished desk. Perhaps at one time my role was necessary but it should never have kept me away from you and Jason. I was wrong! Believe me when I tell you, that is not an easy thing for an old man to admit, especially for a bigoted, opinionated, arrogant and blind old man like your father.
Forgive me son? And believe that I never stopped loving you; I just didn't know how to express my feelings to you or to anyone else. It made me lonely and my loneliness isolated me even more until I reached the point whereat I could not really talk with anyone.

One day something extraordinary happened; a child came to me. He spoke to me of things that only I knew. I know not whence he came or where he went but his message hit hard and I vowed to myself to try to make amends for my stupidity. Yes, stupidity in my blinkered and self-indulgent, self-imposed misery. His message was clear, 'Go to your son,' he said, 'he needs you to be strong for him because he has been given a burden that is terribly hard to bear. Your task is to help him to carry it.'

I didn't understand what he meant but I knew what I must do.

I hope that I have supported you Tomo. I've tried my very best to be a rock for you to cling to. Sometimes I watched you suffer in the secret nocturnal places into which I could not follow, and I wept unashamedly for you, for Jason, for your mother; oh the undeserved pain I must have caused her... and yes, for myself too.

Anna is a blessing. How fortunate are we to have her to care for us? I love her as if she were my own daughter and she has blessed me further with my grandson; little Tod. He has been such a joy to me. Look after them both my boy; they are jewels in your crown and invaluable as such; priceless treasures.

And now it is you to whom I have clung; you who have supported me in my deterioration and dotage. 'Thank you' cannot express the gratitude I feel. At one time I thought I should die alone. However, you are here and will see me through these last few weeks, days, hours. Thank you.

The story? Yes, I am tired my son but not too tired to recognise and remember the wisdom in this moralistic tale.

A professor stood in front of his class and on his desk stood a large, empty coffee jar and two glasses of wine. He asked his students, "What is in the jar?"

"Nothing!" they declared. The professor took from his pocket a number of ping-pong balls with which he proceeded to fill the jar. This time he asked, "Is the jar full?"

"Yes!" they cried, at which he reached under the desk and produced a bag of small marbles. These too he poured into the jar and they settled in the gaps between the ping pong balls until there was no more room. "Now is the jar full?" he enquired.

"Of course!" came the response at which he took out a packet of sand. Once more he tipped some into the jar, gently shaking it as he did so, so that the sand also filled the small spaces between the other contents. This time he did not need to ask.

"Ah! Now it really is full!" They all began to talk at once, laughing and chatting together. He held up his hand for silence; wordlessly they watched in awe as the professor finally picked up the two glasses of wine and poured them into the jar as well.

Do you understand my son? Do you see what that clever professor was demonstrating to his class?

The ping pong balls represent the big things in life; family, health, children, friends and so on. The marbles are the smaller things such as a car, a holiday, your job and your house. The sand is everything else; the little unimportant things with which we fill our lives. You could choose to fill the jar with sand alone but if you do that there will be no room for the marbles or balls; the things that really matter. So you see, if you fill your life with the non-essential, there is no room for the main things. That is what I did Tomo; I sweated the small stuff and left no room for you. But I learned my lesson, I tried to make amends and now I can pass on my knowledge to you and hope that you will understand.

I digress! The wine you ask? What is the wine for? Well that is to remind you to always make time for old friends – so meet them, value them and give of yourself and your time. Have a drink on me!

Never forget what really matters; never lose sight of what is crucial. Anna, Tod and maybe one day grandchildren of your own are central to your own fulfilment. If they are happy then so will you be. Make their happiness your mission.

I love you my son, I am proud of all that you have achieved in the face of almost unbearable adversity. I am with you always.

Dad xxx

It had lain there on the bedside table. Tomo had found the manila envelope with his name emblazoned across it in Harold's well-schooled, slightly shaky, copperplate handwriting. He was quite certain it had not been there earlier. There too, gently laid across the paper, pearly in its white iridescence, perfectly formed, exquisitely perfumed and nestled at its heart, a solitary diamond dewdrop; a single rosebud.

***

The music swelled in sympathy with his heart and the strains of 'The Trumpet Voluntary' broke into his thoughts and brought him abruptly back to the present. Anna pressed her hand into his and smiled up at Tomo, pride pinking her cheeks as she struggled to control the threatening deluge of happy tears.

Chapter Thirty

He had been determined not to attend. It wasn't his thing. He'd feel silly in a suit. There was too much to do at the farm. It was too far to travel in a day and a hotel overnight would be expensive... The excuses came thick and fast but Sally wasn't listening. They were going and that was it; no argument.

***

Sally thought back to the day that she had dreaded; the day of Sandra's visit. She had busied herself all morning while Tom was away to collect his cousin from the station. The cosy farmhouse was spotless, the meal was prepared, she'd changed her outfit at least three times and now she sat trying to concentrate on the embroidered tablecloth that she had picked at from time to time for many years. Would she ever finish it? Her mother had begun the pattern when Sally was just a little tot but time and the pressures of running a farm as well as raising her daughter had meant that it was more often pushed aside and forgotten. Passed from mother to daughter, nowadays it was only brought out when idle fingers needed occupation; this was just such a time.

She was still trying to work out why she felt quite so disturbed when Bruno raised his grizzled head and growled his usual warning. She heard the sound of the Landrover crawling up the narrow lane and put the fabric aside once more before crossing the kitchen flagstones to push the simmering kettle back onto the hottest part of the hob.

***

He need not have been concerned, she really hadn't altered one bit. He'd have recognised her anywhere with her bohemian style flowing skirts, her neat ankle boots, the multi-coloured shawl draped across her shoulders and little wild curls escaping from the bandana wound

142

around her head. She squealed when she saw him and, dropping her scruffy and voluminous bag, raced down the last few yards of the platform and leapt into his arms.

"Hey man, how I've missed you," she panted breathlessly, "I was so scared at the thought of seeing you again. I thought I wouldn't know you, you being a married man and all that, but hey you're no different at all!" She paused for breath and Tom; gently unpeeling her leech like hug, scooped up the abandoned bag, flung it onto his shoulder and took her elbow to guide her to the waiting vehicle. "Not married," he retorted gruffly as he opened the passenger door for her and before he could continue; "Yeah well, might as well be eh old man?" she teased, "So what's she like this Sally of yours?"

She prattled on continuously until they turned into the bottom of the lane which led to Windy Ridge Farm. She was suddenly silenced and Tom glanced at her, "What's up?" he coaxed.

"Will she like me?" Up to that point he had not perceived her lingering insecurity which still simmered just below the surface of her apparent buoyant confidence. Perhaps he should have realised, for all her chatter, she was just as nervous as he was. "Of course she will," he reassured his cousin, "how could anyone not like someone as nice as you?" She blushed, pleased at the unexpected compliment. How things change over time! It was not so long ago that she had behaved very badly in her outrageous flirting and constant demands of her handsome cousin and he had never once reprimanded her. He had been the essence of kindness, if a little distant; but who could blame him for that?

"I'm sorry," she said as the Landrover squelched into the muddy farmyard.

"For what?"

"For the way I behaved when you were always so nice to me." A tear threatened to escape from her carefully made-up eyes.

"Hey, don't start all that!" Tom responded, "It was all done and dusted a long time ago. We've both moved on from those times." It was the most he had said since they met and he gave her a tight hug as he helped her down from the seat. Grabbing her bag from the back seat he grunted, "Whoa! What on earth have you got in here? It weighs a ton!" Laughing once more, she took the bag from him as he ushered her across the yard making sure she did not slip in the mire, "We'll have to find you some wellies instead of those city shoes!" he quipped.

Sally sighed and relaxed as she heard the laughter which heralded the cousins' entrance. She smiled in welcome and held out her hand to the newcomer. Sandra however, after only the briefest moment of hesitation, flung her bag to the floor once more and engulfed Sally in a bearlike hug, her equilibrium restored and her seemingly irrepressible good humour to the fore. Bruno bounced around all three, threatening to knock everything off the coffee table with his wildly thumping flag of a tail. Far too big for the small farm kitchen, he was banished to the yard where he continued to bark his frustration for several more minutes.

Before long the two women were chatting away as though they had known each other for years. Tom slipped out into the yard and he and Bruno rounded up the cattle and brought them in for the evening milking. He breathed in the warm smell of the milking parlour, listened to the gentle hum of the machinery, watched the contented chewing of the cattle, and realised just how lucky he was to have found such an idyllic situation. He silently entreated whatever powers there may be, to let things be; he did not need to have this world turned upside down. And yet he knew that whatever he wished for may well not be what life had in store for him.

It was the name that startled her. Sandra recounted the tale of how she had been helped by a wonderful woman who seemed to know exactly what was needed at any given time. She told the story of the maimed fringe, all those years ago when she was young, wild and foolish. Sally listened in awe, wondering how it was that her own life had seemed so tame in comparison. She laughed delightedly when she heard how Tom had saved the day with his ingenious bandana but gasped in surprise when Sandra described how the hair had seemed to be miraculously restored. The only explanation being that the mysterious woman on the bus had worked some kind of magic. She went on to tell of how the same inscrutable lady had appeared again, many times and usually in some circumstance of crisis, and how she had always poured oil on stormy seas and brought calm and common sense to bear.

"Her name? Bethany." Sandra dismissed the information as irrelevant and prattled on about how it was Bethany who had encouraged her to take up nursing and how much she enjoyed her work now. Nevertheless, Sally breathed in sharply. She knew that name; but why? Where had she heard it before?

The evening passed uneventfully and soon it was time to retire for the night. Sandra had to catch an early train the following morning; she was back on duty for a night shift at the hospital the next day. Sally showed her to the little box room that they had divided from the main sleeping area to create a spare room for visitors. Though truth to tell Sandra was the first visitor to use it and it was mainly filled with the sort of rarely used detritus that most households seem to accumulate. On the makeshift bedside table, an up-ended apple box, was a photograph album and Sandra picked it up and glanced at the dusty and fading pictures.

"Are these your family?" she enquired.

"Some of them are yes," replied Sally, "but I don't know all their names, or how they are related to me." Sandra continued to flick through the pages until as she neared the end of the collection she paused at one and peered more closely at the dimly lit photo. "Oh!" she exclaimed, "I'm sure I've seen this face before." She held the book out to Sally who took it carefully and held it closer to the dim lamp. "I'm afraid I can't make out who that is in this light. Probably some long lost relative or maybe an old beau of my mother's."

Smiling, she dismissed the subject and handed the album back to Sandra, "Good night my dear," she said, "I'm so glad that you found the courage to come. I think I'm already beginning to love you as a cousin-in-law and friend."

"Me too!" declared Sandra as the two women embraced, "Sleep well, Cousin Sally."

***

Next morning, the household awoke early and when Tom returned from the early milking, they breakfasted on porridge, bacon and eggs. "A proper farmhouse breakfast!" declared Sandra with her mouth full of toast. Without waiting for acknowledgement from either of her hosts she went on, "Oh, and by the way, that man in the photograph? I remembered just as I was falling asleep. I'm pretty sure he was my father's uncle. I think his name was Great Uncle Dan or Danny, or something like that. Although the funny thing is I seem to recall Mum saying that he had died in the war. I guess that must have been the First World War? Anyway, it's strange that he should be in your album." Pausing to take another sip of tea, she thought no more about it. She crammed the last bite of toast into her mouth and mumbled through the crumbs as she drew from her pocket the carefully wrapped gift that she had forgotten about the day before.

"I brought you this." She proffered the package to Tom, "I hope you like it." He took it and unwrapped the unusual paperweight. He was stunned to see the rose; preserved in all its glory. He knew immediately where and when he had seen it before and he looked intently into Sandra's eyes. She gazed back unwaveringly and then they both turned to Sally who was staring at the gift and looking equally amazed. She too had seen this bloom before. Nothing was said; words were not necessary, and silence prevailed as Sandra collected up the last of her belongings and followed Tom out to the waiting Landrover.

"Thank you!" called Sally to the retreating vehicle and as she turned to go back into the warmth of the old kitchen, she caught the faintest whiff of an exquisite perfume.

Later that morning, and before Tom had returned from the station, she remembered the photograph. Mounting the rickety stairs she entered the small bedroom. First she opened the curtains, then she remade the bed, and only after she'd tidied the shelves and replaced the borrowed items did she cautiously take up the album. It opened easily at the appointed page, and there looking out at her, clearly discernible in the bright morning light, was the face she had known so well and had, in the short time she'd known him, come to love as a surrogate father figure. Daniel; Daniel and Dora, her saviours and the whole reason for her being right here, right now and oh so very alright. Coincidence? Maybe there is no such thing as coincidence. Maybe this is all preordained, predetermined; a future mapped out for us over which we have little if any control. She was puzzled but also at peace. She knew that these ripples were panning out just as they should and she understood that sometimes things happen that leave us incredulous. Then she remembered the other coincidence that had shaken her equilibrium yesterday. She crossed into the main bedroom and rummaged in the pocket of her old, now discarded, anorak. Her fingers found the forgotten folded; slightly scrumpled paper and she pulled it out, smoothed it out and read again the name of her Good Samaritan from many years earlier. Bethany. No surname, just Bethany and a partial address that she did not recognise.

Chapter Thirty-One

Bethany stood at the back of the small chapel. As always she was smartly dressed in black from head to foot. Round her neck was a delicate silver chain from which hung an ornate pendant crafted into a diamond centred rose, and in her hand was the smaller hand of a young, blonde curly haired boy. Holding the other hand of the same youth was Elsa.

***

The organ thundered out Clarke's "Trumpet Voluntary" and all heads turned to see the entrance of the bride in all her finery. Tod faltered; stunned not only by the beauty of his bride, but also by what he saw next. His smile froze into a ghastly grimace, as he witnessed his wife-to-be fling her arms around a tall, handsome stranger who was waiting just inside the chapel doors. She kissed him passionately and profusely. Jealousy surged through Tod's veins and his hands shook violently. He was about to sit down abruptly, or perhaps take flight via a side door, or at the very least cry out in anguish, when he felt the firm hand of his father on his shoulder. The grip was relentless and Tod was going nowhere. He watched in astonishment as his mother left her seat and walked to the embracing couple; her footsteps ringing out in the echoing silence. Mutterings began amongst the few guests and they all gazed in shocked surprise as the scene unfolded before them.

Anna reached Sandra's side and looked at her hesitantly and questioningly. Suddenly Sandra's strong, infectious laugh rang out through the nave of the Chapel and everyone visibly relaxed and nervously smiled one to another. Tomo's grip was released as Tod's feet remained firmly fixed to the floor.

"I'd like you all to meet my cousin, Tom!" Sandra announced, "He's my only living relative and I love him. He has agreed to give me away."

Someone began to clap and quickly others joined in. Soon, the usually peaceful sanctuary, that was the sombre Chapel, was transformed with laughing, cheering and applause. Tod was folded into his father's arms and briefly leaned his head on his shoulder. Tomo patted his back and understood. Equilibrium restored, congregation calmed and the organ began to bellow out a wedding march.

Anna took from her bag an exquisite white single stem rose and carefully pushed into the centre of the posy of riotously coloured flowers that Sandra held. She looked deeply into Sandra's eyes, loved what she saw there, and returned to her place beside her husband. As she turned she glanced at the small group of people standing near the back. She recognised only the young lad whose impish grin was unmistakeable. She did not question his presence but smiled and nodded very slightly in acknowledgement. As she turned away she thought she saw him wink in return but when she looked back she could see none of the three.

***

Afterwards, when pondering on the extraordinary proceedings of the day, Tomo realised that he knew the dark austere lady standing with the pretty woman and the young boy. It was none other than Nurse Isabella, without whom he might not have been here at all. He had looked for the three after the service; after the, 'Will you, Tod...' at which a ripple of laughter ran through the church, 'I mean Harold Jason Thomson take Alexandra Agatha McKay to be your lawful wedded wife?' and the 'I will's and 'I do's which had threatened to reduce him to unmanly tears, but there was no sign of them anywhere.

Later that same night, as he lay in comfortable insomnia after he and Anna had tenderly made love, with a shock he realised that he had also met the lad before, albeit a younger version. Nevertheless there was no mistaking those bright blue eyes and curly blonde hair.

There are some things in life that are seemingly inexplicable and this was one of those conundrums. He wasn't disturbed by the appearance of the woman and the boy; he was puzzled. Above all, he was filled with a sense of completeness, of balance and fulfilment and he knew that somehow, although probably he would never know exactly how, things were working out just as they should and that these people, who had dropped in and out of his life, had something to do with the 'all-right-ness' of it all. He found himself thinking of his father and his brother and as he drifted off into a deep slumber, he breathed in the exquisite perfume that he remembered so well.

**

Sally lay curled into Tom's back, breathing in the scent of him and feeling his warmth on her skin. She was content, although the unfamiliar hotel room denied her sleep. However, relaxed and satisfied she reviewed the day's events. She had worried about the secrecy and, truth to tell, uncertainty about their attendance at the wedding. It had taken all her powers of persuasion to get Tom to agree to be there and superhuman strength to persuade him to give his cousin away. Nevertheless, it had all worked wonderfully well. She had also been concerned about what reaction the groom might have had to their unexpected appearance and initially she had been right. Tod was visibly shaken but he had quickly regained his composure and she admired him for that.

The only remaining puzzles of the day were the three strangers who were not strangers at all. How she knew Bethany, she could not tell and despite never consciously having met her before, she instantly recognised her former saviour. Bethany had smiled and nodded at her and she in response had mouthed the words, "Thank you!" intending to make a much more formal greeting after the officialdom was over.

The boy, she knew. She remembered him standing by her bed in the hospital and she remembered him in the kitchen at the farm. She could not recollect how he came to be in either of those places although she clearly remembered the messages he had carried.

150

"How very strange things can be..." she mused as tiredness overcame her and her eyelids refused to remain open a minute longer. She slept.

***

There was no sleep at all for Sandra! Married? Married! It had not really sunk in until the hotel receptionist had referred to her as Mrs Thomson. Repressing an almost irresistible urge to giggle, she had responded in the affirmative whilst leaning possessively against Tod's body. He smiled down at her and moved his hand from her shoulder, stroking gently but firmly down her spine to her buttocks which he lightly pinched; a promise of delights to follow.

The delights were indeed delightful, as always, and Tod snored softly beside her as she smiled at the recollection of the look on his face when Tom had appeared at the Chapel. She giggled quietly and Tod stirred, murmuring unintelligibly in his sleep.

It hadn't been Tom's presence alone that had so delighted her. At first she had not noticed Bethany and the other two strangers and it was only as they returned from signing the register and began their triumphant exit down the aisle that she recognised her friend and mentor. She beamed at Bethany who smiled and nodded in return until Sandra's attention was diverted by the well wishes of other guests. When at last she had a moment to look again, Bethany, the lad and the other visitor were nowhere to be seen.

Sandra looked sleepily across the room at the beautiful bouquet lying on the dressing table; tomorrow, in the absence of a bridesmaid to catch it, they would take the flowers to lay on her parents' grave. She missed them. As a single tear, not of sorrow but of deep, deep joy, rolled down her cheek, she watched its diamond twin roll from the centre of the white rose which took pride of place in the arrangement.

***

151

Earlier in the day, just before the end of the simple service and as the triumphal wedding march resounded from the small but ancient organ, three figures had glided silently across the courtyard and into the park which had previously been the training ground for many thousands of soldiers. The short soft grass, damp with summer rain, bore no witness to their passing. At the far side of the field the taller woman broke away and having briefly embraced the younger two, was soon lost to sight. The moist heat of the day dissipated into a mist which soon obscured the two remaining figures. And there was no sound; there was no substance; there was nothing.

Chapter Thirty-Two

The shrill 'dring' of the doorbell pierced the stillness of the late January afternoon rousing her from her habitual after lunch snooze. Startled, Eleanor rose stiffly from her comfortable recliner and silently thanked the technological wonders of the amazing chair which pushed her gently upright. Making her way slowly across the room, she wondered who on earth it could be. She wasn't anticipating visitors and fully expected to see a salesman or Jehovah's Witnesses standing at her door. Fumbling with the lock and chain that Simon had insisted she use when home alone, she was astonished when the door burst open and a shabbily dressed woman pushed past her into the immaculate hallway. "'Bout time too!" came the gruff and abruptly rude remark, "'S'not nice to keep people waiting when it's so bloomin' cold out 'ere." Eleanor was lost for words. Her mouth opened and closed but no sounds emanated from her lips. "Well, aren't you goin' to offer an old lady a cuppa?" continued the newcomer and before Eleanor could respond she added, "I'm Lucy by the way." For a second or two Eleanor's mind was a blank and then, as realisation and recognition swept over her, she recovered her innate composure and, "I'm so sorry, of course you must come in and welcome I'm sure," she said.

For some strange reason it didn't occur to Eleanor to wonder why she was apologising to this almost stranger when in reality it was the intruder who had offended the niceties of etiquette. Nevertheless, she graciously offered her hand and after her initial surprise at the absence of a hand to shake in response, she took the coat that was thrust into it and laid it carefully over the back of a nearby chair. Lucy followed her into the kitchen and made herself at home by plonking her rather broad backside onto a waiting breakfast stool. "Milk and two sugars," she demanded and proceeding to take out from her capacious bag a rusting tobacco tin, began to roll a cigarette. Eleanor was at a loss. What should she do first? Fetch an ash tray? Put the kettle on? Ask questions? Tell her to leave? Realising she had little choice she quickly assessed the situation and filled the kettle and switched it on. Next she found a saucer to act as an ashtray but Lucy pushed it aside saying, "Don' worry; I'll take meself outside wiv me fag." Eleanor relaxed a little. At least that would give her a minute or two to collect herself and maybe send Elsa a quick text asking her to hurry home with the shopping.

Perfunctory introductions completed, cigarette smoked; outside as promised, and tea tray prepared, Eleanor reluctantly invited Lucy into her personal lounge area; her inner sanctum, the privacy of which was respected by all members of the household, except the feline and canine residents. Almost blind and partially deaf, Snowball growled fiercely at the odorous figure until Eleanor soothed him with a pat and the reassurance that this person was 'allowed'. However, he continued to grumble quietly to himself and fixed Lucy with an unblinking stare with which he threatened her to not make any kind of attack on his beloved mistress.

"Well this is fancy in't it?" said Lucy, "No wonder 'e likes it 'ere. Not a patch on wot me and my girl could've offered 'im."

"We are very lucky." Eleanor was wondering what exactly Lucy wanted and as if reading her thoughts Lucy continued, "I 'aven't come to cause any trouble. I know the boy is 'appy 'ere an' I'm not about to spoil that for 'im. You might find it 'ard to believe, but I love the boy. I jus' wan' ter be sure 'e's alright; wiv 'is 'ealth an' all that. I know 'e's 'ad problems an' that's why I wanted 'is gran'dad to 'elp 'im. I didn' know 'e was ill 'imself and then when 'e went an' died I wanted ter see for meself where me grandson was livin' and 'oo you people are."

Eleanor began to understand that despite her rough manner and appearance, here was a woman with a good heart and who loved her daughter and grandson. She relaxed a little as she poured the tea and proffered a plate of muffins baked by Carrie earlier that morning.

Thus, it was that sometime later when Elsa and Carrie arrived home with the shopping, they found Eleanor and Lucy poring over the family photograph album and laughing together at the antics of the two boys. Eleanor explained a little about Timothy's petit mal and told Lucy how wonderful Thomas had been at watching and protecting Timothy during his episodes. Snowball drew nearer to the scruffy lady and soon his head was resting on her foot as she absently scratched behind his ears. "I remember a lovely lady wot Phillip used ter mention sometimes. 'Er name was Tammy or somefin like that. 'E said she used ter go a bit strange sometimes. Do yer fink it's the same fing?" For a moment she was taken aback with surprise; this woman knew Phillip better than she had realised. After a brief silence, during which she swallowed the unexpected lump which threatened to transform into tears, Eleanor replied, "No, I think not." She paused again, "Tam was my niece. She was a very special person but she is no blood relation to Timothy..."

"Don' 'ave ter be in the blood!" interrupted Lucy, with surprising depth of insight, "sometimes it's in the loving."

With that she rose to her feet and gathering up her voluminous bag, she rummaged in its depths for a moment. "I 'ave ter be on me way now," she announced abruptly, "but I would like you ter give this ter the boy if yer wouldn' min'. Me girl made it in that 'ome they've got 'er shut away in. It's awright there but I'd rather 'ave 'er 'at 'ome wiv me. On'y I couldn't cope wiv 'er when she 'as one of 'er turns. She gets a bit wild and she's bloody strong too! She don' usually mention the boy but one day she tol' me she'd 'ad a dream 'an then she picked this in the garden at the 'ome. She made it for 'im. I like ter fink she knows 'e's awright 'ere wiv you lot." She held out a roughly wrapped package, "It's 'eavy!" she smiled, "I'll be glad not ter 'ave ter take it back wiv me!"

As Eleanor hesitated, Lucy placed the parcel on the coffee table and shrugged. She shuffled to the hallway and retrieved her coat. Almost before Eleanor could recover her composure she was at the door and fumbling with the catch. "G'bye then." she said.

155

"But don't you want to see Thomas?" Eleanor quickly enquired, "He'll be home in about half an hour."

"Nah!" Lucy replied, "It's better I don' see 'im. 'E's 'appy 'an it'd on'y make me sad..." she sniffed wetly and wiped her sleeve across her eyes. "Ta for everyfink." and pulling the tobacco tin from her pocket, "You'll give 'im the thingy?" she asked. "Tell 'im 'is mum an' gran love 'im." And she was gone. All that was left was a vague whiff of tobacco and the sweet, sickly smell of a too long unwashed body.

***

Thomas stared unseeing out of the uncurtained window into the pitch black night beyond. Not naturally a deep thinker, he generally accepted what came his way and paid little heed to things over which he had no control. The only things that ever upset his equilibrium were Timothy's 'episodes', to which in truth he was getting used, and anything involving the ancient Peanut whose health was seriously declining. Nevertheless, the news of his grandmother's visit had disturbed him and he wasn't at all sure why she had come.

The door crashed open and Timothy made his usual unannounced and unceremonious entrance. "What's up bro?" he enquired as he punched his best friend perfunctorily on the shoulder. Thomas feigned a fall before swinging his fist softly into Timothy's belly, "Nothing's up!" he responded.

"Then why are you down?" Timothy chuckled at his own quip.

"Not down! Just thinking..."

"Hey careful man, that's a dangerous thing to do you know!" Timothy's irrepressible good humour made Thomas smile and before long they were watching a film and munching on homemade popcorn provided by the ever attentive Carrie who still considered the half adult boys as her charges.

An hour or so later she came to chivvy them to bed despite that they were quite capable of realising the time and the necessity to be up for college the next morning. They good naturedly teased her and pretended refusal until she crossly stamped her foot while Snowball yapped and Peanut lazily sauntered out of the way to the safety of Thomas' bed. Into this cacophony came Eleanor. She laughed and soothed and quieted the party until calm was restored. As the boys were still grinning at each other and Carrie was softly grumbling to herself, Eleanor held out the scruffy package to Thomas. He looked up at her questioningly and she told him how his grandmother had said it was from his mother, of her dream and that she wanted him to have this gift.

At first he had been dismayed that she had not waited to see him but as he thought over all that Eleanor had told him, he began to understand how it might have been painful for her. She had, to all intents and purposes lost her daughter and her grandson but, to her credit, she had made a life for herself. It is all too easy to criticise others for their choices in life but we can never know what it is like to walk in someone else's shoes. He made a mental note to himself to visit his grandmother at some point in the future. After all he had much for which to be grateful to her.

He didn't notice Timothy slip away to his room across the landing. He picked up the package and unwrapped the crumpled paper to reveal a heavy resin paperweight. He gazed into its depth and wondered. Encased in a transparent bubble, in all its perfectly formed pearly white iridescence nestled a single rose and at its centre a sparkling diamond dewdrop.

Chapter Thirty-Three

Would it be today? How could anyone concentrate on work when such a life-changing occurrence was imminent?

Tod greeted the next patient in his usual polite manner. This one was a familiar client. The boy had been brought to him as a toddler. Born with one foot grossly deformed, the decision had been made to amputate soon after birth and so the child never missed what he had never had. Over the years, as he grew, a prosthetic limb had been adjusted and remoulded and remade so as to accommodate his needs. Tod took pride in his work and satisfaction from seeing his partially incapacitated customers pleased with his solutions to their problems. He supposed it was inevitable that he would enjoy his chosen career. After all he had grown up with a father who had a prosthetic leg and who was constantly tweaking and adjusting the limb that he had designed himself. It was Tomo's leg that had inspired his desire to help other people in similar situations. That combined with his aptitude for electronic and micro technology had resulted in him gaining a reputation for excellence in his field. Nevertheless, he was not proud but humbled rather to be able to give independence and a degree of freedom to those that came to him in need.

However, today he was on edge and he was glad to be able to close the surgery door behind the last patient on his list for the morning. The afternoon would be spent in his workshop and that he could leave at any moment should the anticipated call come.

***

Unable to settle to anything Anna donned her windcheater and wellies and, whistling to Billy who heaved himself to his arthritic feet and wagged his tail perfunctorily, she set off to walk across the field behind the parade grounds. The strong wind buffeted her slight figure and she leaned into the headwind, thankful for the distraction of keeping from falling. Billy plodded stoically beside her; gone were the days when he would have been racing across the fields ahead of her, chasing his own tail and all the imaginary adversaries that needed to be hunted down and 'killed'.

Would today be the day she wondered? Due dates were a bit of an imprecise science despite the wonders of modern medical development. In her opinion, babies came when they were ready and that was that! She was delighted to become a grandmother, although astonished that she was apparently old enough to be one. Surely it was only a little while ago that she became a mother? She smiled wryly to herself and wiped away a tear that the wind had brought to her eye....

***

Tomo leaned back in the old brown leather armchair. After all these years he finally understood what it was that his father had enjoyed about this room. Its oak panelling, high ceiling, the huge bay window and the heavy old-fashioned furniture gave it an air of austerity but it also had an odd, timeless comfortability about it. The fire roaring in the grate in all seasons, the two big old armchairs either side of the fireplace, the books lining the walls, the thick pile hearth rug and the polished coffee table, were as familiar to him as his own hands and there was satisfaction and reassurance to be taken from such familiarity.

His reverie was broken by the shrill sound of the telephone. One concession to modernisation had been the installation of wireless phones throughout the house. Often, in the past, the hall phone had rung and the call been missed through the impossibility of getting to the handset in time. Therefore, the 'new' system had proved itself invaluable and Tomo grinned in satisfaction as he reached to respond to its summons.

***

Sally sat and sewed. It was unusual for her to sit at this time of day and unusual for her to be focused on her embroidery for any length of time. But today she couldn't concentrate on anything else. The soft package was neatly wrapped ready for the call, the evening casserole was bubbling in the slow cooker, the bread rolls ready to bake and an apple pie waited only for custard. As she sewed she pondered on the future. Who would have thought that she would be waiting for news such as this?

***

Tom was impatient to be home. The cattle seemed to take forever to make their way back up the lane. They ambled slowly and unconcerned, stopping to pull mouthfuls of the long grass from the verge or deliberately turning in the wrong gateway. Meg, the collie, nipped at their hocks and chivvied them along but they were going to go at their own pace and nothing or no one would hurry them today. He wasn't sure why he was so keen to hear the news. It wasn't as though it would make a great difference to his daily routine but it was somehow a milestone in his life. One that he and Sally had accepted was unlikely to happen for them. They were content and happy as they were and they were delighted to be able to share in the good fortune of those that they loved. Grandparents they would not be but they could be the best Grand Cousins anyone had ever had!

***

At 17.43 hours precisely, on a blustery March day, Tamara Miriam Thomson, made her entrance into the world.

***

Her labour had been long, although not as hard as she had feared it might be. All the way through she had had a sense of purpose. She rode the waves of pain as a surfer rides the sea and the exhilaration of the ultimate push was akin to a climber reaching the pinnacle of his mountain. Finally, in her arms was placed the part of her that she had carried in her belly for the last nine months. She already adored this tiny person; eyes tightly closed, fists tightly clenched, mouth firmly clamped on her mother's breast, she was perfect and Sandra was never going to let her go. Nevertheless, the euphoria in holding her daughter close to her heart could not assuage her need for sleep and as the motherly midwife tenderly lifted the babe from her arms, she sank into the exhausted and satisfied sleep that is the reward for hard labour.

Tod gazed down at the tiny sleeping form. The bleeps from monitors and the snuffles and small cries from other babies that had nothing to do with him, faded into the background as he focused on his daughter. Mari, he would call her Mari...

A light touch on his shoulder startled him and as he turned he found himself looking into a pair of piercing blue eyes. The golden haired child smiled into him as he stood shoulder to shoulder with the seated Tod. There were no words; communication was silent. The child held out his small pink palm whereon rested a polished golden pebble hung on a silver chain. He nodded towards the crib and placed the pebble in Tod's larger and rougher hand. Curling the strong fingers around the gift, Timothy smiled. He bent to the crib and placed a hand on the soft copper down of her head and gently kissed Mari's forehead. "See you later," he whispered and was gone.

***

"Oh but it's absolutely exquisite!" exclaimed Sandra. The silvery white gossamer shawl, with its embossed rose centre, shimmered in its delicacy as Sandra laid it carefully across the sleeping baby's form. How had Sally found the time to make such a gift with its intricate yet bold pattern? Her rough, farmer's wife exterior belied her penchant for fine things and her artistic ability to create such magnificence with needles and yarn. Sandra kissed her cousin-in-law and the two heads bent again to admire the work, the beauty and the baby.

161

"Tamara is such a pretty name," said Sally, "and I love the abbreviation to Mari, it sort of ties it in with Miriam too!" she paused while she gently stroked the sleeping baby's cheek. She ran her finger lightly under Mari's chin and up across her forehead, "Isn't this little birthmark adorable? It looks just like a kiss!" Mari stirred and grimaced and the two women drew back a little. Sandra swept up the shawl and laid it out to refold and put aside for the time being. It would be saved for the christening since it was far too nice for everyday use!

Later, when Sally was about to leave, she remembered to ask, "Why Miriam?" Sandra smiled, "My mother used to talk fondly of her Aunt Miriam and Uncle Ted. I always liked the name! I thought about calling her Agatha after my mum, but it's a harsh name for such a soft sweet child and in any case it is my middle name, so I gave her Great Aunt Miriam's – it means 'star of the sea' in Hebrew but there are other meanings given, one of which is 'she who knows' and another is 'rebellion'. I suppose it is a sort of bittersweet name and I hope it means she will be strong, beautiful, clever and compassionate."

"I'm sure she will..." murmured Sally and for some strange reason she was suddenly reminded of Dora and Daniel, those enigmatic people who had supported her so magnificently in her hour of need.

Chapter Thirty-Four

"Is she there?" Thomas puffed as he hurried round the last corner. Miles behind Timothy, he squinted into the sun as he endeavoured to see who was or wasn't at the bus stop today. He rubbed his eyes as he drew level with the shelter and wiped away the annoying tears that invariably made it look as though he was upset when he was not. Once again he reminded himself to ask Elsa's opinion; he really couldn't see as well as he used to, perhaps he needed glasses? Sometimes his eyes just refused to focus although the shades that he had borrowed from Timothy did make a difference. He hadn't borrowed them for that of course; he had hoped they might make him look a little more sophisticated and suave. At nineteen, he was suddenly conscious of his shortcomings in the looks department. He was still rather plump and of course his condition meant that he was always either very pale or very red if he failed to protect himself from the sun. At times his skin seemed almost transparent and he had got into the habit of always wearing long trousers and long sleeves. They, together with the hat that Eleanor insisted he wear in the sun, were extremely 'uncool' in his opinion but for the most part he was unconcerned with his appearance. He knew he would never be as eye-catchingly attractive as Timothy.

He plonked himself down on the wooden bench and looked up at Timothy who was lounging lazily against the post which bore the bus stop sign. Smiling into Timothy's eyes, totally oblivious to the new arrival, the copper topped girl was absorbed in the story with which he was currently regaling her. Thomas sighed and pulled from his bag his ubiquitous novel and settled himself to wait for the bus. He frowned to himself as the words blurred on the page. He really must ask Elsa to make him an appointment with the optician.

He closed the book and his eyes. They always arrived here much too soon and he fully realised that the real reason was for Timothy to spend as much time as possible chatting up this particular girl. It had taken him weeks to raise enough courage to say hello but now there was no stopping him. Thomas sighed; how he wished there was a girl who was as absorbed in him as this one was in his brother. Nevertheless, he wouldn't dwell on it; his placid good nature allowed him to take pleasure in other people's happiness and none more so than this friend-come-brother.

Perhaps it was his unusually self-focused reverie, or perhaps it was because of his failing eyesight that he didn't notice the familiar signs, but a cry and the thump of falling bag caused him to turn sharply to where Timothy had been leaning and laughing. He leapt to his feet and caught Timothy just as he crumpled in a shaking heap; his limbs jerking and head twisting as the fit flooded through him. Ignoring the girl who hovered anxiously beside him, asking irrelevant questions and offering to fetch help, he sat and cradled Timothy until the spasms receded and his body relaxed. He laid him gently on the ground and having checked for minor injuries, pulled his limbs into the recovery position. He retrieved the dropped rucksack, laid his jacket over the prostrate form and sat back down on the bench to wait.

To her credit, Mari had remained silent. Realising that Thomas was in control of the situation and that this was obviously a regular occurrence, she waited too. After a short while she spoke softly, "Does he do that often?" Thomas looked up, surprised since he had almost forgotten that she was there.

"Oh!" he responded, "Yes, well no, not that often... sometimes..." he muttered, his tongue tripping over the words now that she was actually speaking to him. Although she had always acknowledged his presence with a nod and a smile, she only had eyes and words for Timothy. However, Thomas was quite used to being the pale shadow behind his enigmatic and gregarious pal, and bore neither him nor her ill will. He wasn't sure how much Timothy would want him to impart to this girl and so he was guarded in his response and told her the barest minimum of detail, reassuring her that he would be fine and would wake up very soon. He might not even remember what had happened.

164

As he finished speaking, a bus came trundling around the corner and she stood up to hail it to stop. This was her bus, not the one that Thomas and Timothy would have caught for she now went to the college on the other side of town. Despite that they had only spent a few minutes at the bus stop twice weekly on the days that their lectures coincided, all three were conscious of a bond forming between them. "Tell him I hope he's ok?" she sounded concerned, "and I hope I'll see you all on Friday?" the lift in her voice made it a question and Thomas nodded perfunctorily, "Yes, I expect he'll be fine then." He looked down and brushed a wisp of hair away from Timothy's eye and when he looked up again, the bus and the girl were gone. It was some time later, when suddenly realising that he too was included in her hopes for Friday, and he smiled softly to himself, under no illusion whatsoever of her real hope.

* * *

The figures swirled around him and he could make out none of the faces. Sounds were muffled and it was almost as though he was floating through a mist so thick that it blanketed out reality. Occasionally someone or something came close and leant over him, took his wrist or touched his forehead. He could not have explained where he was or what was happening. However, he was unconcerned; he felt safe, he felt warm and he knew that whatever was taking place was just as it should be. Sometimes he thought he could make out whispered words but they meant nothing and he wasn't at all sure they were in the language he understood. Nevertheless he did understand that it was all for him.

When at last a figure he recognised stood beside him and took his hand, he was not surprised to see her. In her arms she held something small, white, fluffy and very still. He understood that it was his time; that he could no longer warn and protect. He reached out a hand, which seemed detached from the rest of him and moved independent of thought on his part, and he pressed his fingers into the soft, silky hair. He thought he smiled, he thought he spoke thanking her for

165

lending him to him, he thought a farewell and he thought how he would miss his canine companion. He thought...

She turned away from him and another hooded figure, cloaked in black, took the small silvery bundle from her arms. For a second he raised his head and Timothy found himself gazing into a pair of piercing blue eyes...

***

Thomas was worried. There would be no lectures for him today. Two buses had come and gone and still Timothy slept. He didn't usually take this long to awake and when he eventually stirred and tried to sit up, his body twisted and cramped again. Thomas held him once more until the spasms subsided, a little more quickly this time, and laid him on his side for a second time. He pushed the rucksack into the small of his back to prevent him from rolling over and reluctantly, although with little choice, he set off home to fetch help. He had never quite got into the habit of carrying with him his mobile phone and he chastised himself for his failure to foresee its need today.

The ambulance was summoned by Elsa, whose cool demeanour and sensible manner calmed Thomas who was agitated beyond measure. She dispatched him to hurry back to the bus stop with a blanket and told him to stay with Timothy until help arrived. Before leaving herself, she slipped into Eleanor's room where she found the older lady cradling Snowball in her arms. Tears slid slowly down the wrinkled cheeks but a watery smile eased the sorrow. "It was quick and easy for him," she whispered and Elsa nodded in acknowledgement of the message behind the words. She did not trouble Eleanor with Timothy's plight, there would be time enough for that and his life was not in danger. This she knew for certain for she knew that his path was not ended yet.

As Thomas, puffing even more mightily than before, came round the final bend he was puzzled to see two figures lying together where he had left just one. As he drew nearer he could see that Timothy had not moved and was still lying with his back facing the direction from which he came. Yet surely there is something else there? Thomas cursed his poor eyes and almost ran the last few steps to the body. He sank to his knees and was surprised and shocked to hear a low cautionary growl. A smooth black head was raised up from Timothy's side and Thomas looked into the bluest eyes he had ever seen. A pink tongue protruded from the slavering mouth and, recognising that this was friend not foe, a black tail thumped softly on the ground.

Chapter Thirty-Five

"Six weeks? I can't stay here that long!" declared Timothy. Already bored and fed up with his imprisonment, he was champing at the bit to get back to living his normal life. Truth to tell he really wanted to get back to the bus stop. He was terrified that he had frightened her off for ever. Curse this damned disease! Not for the first time he wished his malady away. Despite his visit to Old Bess and the vague memory he had of her message; in reality he couldn't remember the words at all, only the message behind them. "All is as it should be." Well he didn't think that this is as it should be, in fact he was quite determined that this is how it should not be. Oh, Thomas was good at keeping him up to date with the events at home and in college; the family's comings and goings and the puppy that had attached itself to him. He mused about the dog; how strange it was that it should appear at precisely the moment Eleanor had witnessed Snowball's demise. Of course he was sad and he wasn't ashamed to have shed a few tears, but Snowball was nearly twenty, just a little older than himself; it was astonishing that he had lived so long. Yet still he puzzled about the newcomer and in that moment he named him; Enigma.

For weeks already, Timothy had undergone test after test. He had been incarcerated in the big London hospital ever since that fateful day at the bus stop. The tests were inconclusive.

Finally, the day had come when the family were called together to discuss the situation. Rosa, Simon, Eleanor and Elsa arrived at the hospital without Thomas who elected to stay behind with Enigma who had developed the habit of chewing things up when no one was at home. Dr Richards began to explain, "Many people with epilepsy can experience changes in the pattern, frequency and nature of their seizures. Such changes might mean a worsening of the disorder, improvement of the condition, or have no consequences." He paused and glanced at Timothy before continuing, "Increase in frequency of seizures might be a sign of worsening of the condition. However, we have seen no indication of this being the case here. Generally speaking Timothy is a very healthy specimen with no obvious issues." Eleanor smiled across the room and Timothy grinned back. It was hard to suppress his natural good humour for long.

"Rarely, psychological stresses and possibly problems in coping with these stresses have caused psychogenic non-epileptic seizures that can super-impose on epileptic seizures making them seem more severe than they actually are." It was difficult to take in all the long words and realising this Dr Richards gave them a moment to absorb the information. Simon took Rosa's hand and absentmindedly stroked the back of it with his thumb. She squeezed his hand in return and without letting go, he smiled reassuringly at her.

"One of the tests sometimes used to help diagnose epilepsy is a brain scan. Sometimes we use an MRI scan and sometimes CT. Are you familiar with these acronyms?" he waited momentarily as they all nodded in the affirmative. "Although they use different technology, both produce an image of the brain which may show a specific cause for epilepsy. We'd like to perform an MRI scan with Timothy." Again he paused but no one interrupted or deferred. He continued, "Depending on what we find there are various available courses of action. I'd like to outline these to you now so that you can consider the options before we need to make a decision." Elsa moved closer to Timothy who had turned a little pale, "What do they mean?" he whispered. She put her finger to her lips and mouthed, "Shhh! We'll talk about it later."

"As you know, since they began to become more severe, which is quite normal in adolescence, we have controlled Timothy's fits with drugs. It may be that all we need to do is to alter the regime but I fear that it may not be that simple. If that is the case then there are different kinds of epilepsy surgery." Eleanor gave a little gasp and Rosa's grip on Simon's hand tightened. "One kind of surgery involves removing a specific area of the brain which is thought to be causing the seizures. Another kind involves separating the part of the brain that is causing seizures from the rest of the brain. It sounds

169

rather alarming," he added as Timothy abruptly stood up, "but for some people surgery can reduce the number of seizures they have and for others they stop altogether."

Timothy stumbled out of the room closely followed by Elsa. As Rosa rose to accompany them, Eleanor's voice commanded her imperiously to stop. "Wait," she said, more gently now that Rosa had obeyed, "Let Dr Richards finish his explanation. It's probably better that we hear it first. Elsa will take care of Timothy."

"Known causes can include scarring on the brain, malformations of brain development, that is problems in how the brain forms, or damage to the brain from a head injury, or following an infection such as meningitis."

"Oh!" gasped Rosa, "Do you remember that time on the Rugby pitch? Perhaps..." Sentence half-finished, she buried her face in Simon's shoulder, "I never wanted him to play that dreadful game!" she mumbled into the fabric of his sweater.

Dr Richards waited for a moment or two and then, "If a specific cause is found, it is called an 'epileptogenic lesion' which can be different in each person." He went on, "If the surgeons can reach the lesion during surgery and can remove it safely without causing new problems; that is without upsetting other parts of the brain such as speech, sight or movement, he will have a good chance of having the seizures stopped by the surgery." Simon let out a long sigh as if he had been holding his breath throughout. "Will there be more tests first?" he asked.

"Yes, of course," came the reply, "he is already here at the specialist centre and some of the tests have already been carried out. We've discussed the MRI and he may have an EEG and we may use a trace chemical injection which can show detailed information about where the seizures start in the brain. Memory and psychological tests are also used to see how his memory and lifestyle might be affected after the surgery. These types of tests also help the doctors to see how he is likely to cope with the impact of having this sort of surgery."

"What is the time scale for all of this?" asked Eleanor, her voice a little quaky.

"As I already indicated, some of the preparation has already been done. Assuming the test results are as we expect and any lesion uncomplicated, we would expect to operate at the end of this week. There is no guarantee of a lesion however." Ignoring this addition, "And when can we take him home afterwards?" Rosa was anxious to have her boy back in her home as soon as possible. Dr Richards explained, "For the first few days he may feel very tired and need to sleep, as it can take a while for the anesthetic to completely wear off. Some people who have brain surgery will have seizures within the first week of surgery although this doesn't necessarily mean that the surgery has not been successful. Seizures after surgery can happen because of the direct stress the brain experiences in surgery, rather than because a person has a history of epilepsy."

At this point, Elsa slipped back into the room, without Timothy who had elected to go back to his hospital room. His head pounding and his heart racing, he was inordinately and inexplicably alarmed at the idea of surgery. Besides he wanted out of this place.

"How long he may need to spend in hospital will depend on the type of surgery he has and how we feel he is recovering. Generally he might expect to be back to his normal activities about six weeks after surgery."

***

It felt like a prison sentence. Not just the terrifying thought of having his brain operated on, but the idea of spending six or more weeks doing not very much. Life was turning upside down. In addition to all that, what about Mari? Surely she would go off with someone else after all that long absence and she is so very attractive... Even Thomas fancies her! Thomas. Timothy screwed up his face at the thought of his best friend; he really should get those eyes checked out...

Chapter Thirty-Six

Upside down? Inside out, back to front and completely screwed up! That's what it was. Thomas? Dead? NO! His whole body screamed denial. It was he who had undergone the dangerous surgery, he who had risked losing his faculties, how could this be? It was an accident they said; he didn't see it coming, no one had realised just how poor his sight had become... EXCUSES! There had to be a better reason, there had to be someone to blame. How could no one have noticed? And the overriding, guilty anger at Thomas himself; WHY? Why did he not tell anyone that he couldn't see? The stupid, stupid boy!

Timothy silently ranted and railed. Cocooned in his hospital room, he could speak to no one and was visited by no one since everyone was in such a state of shock and thought only of him being safely tucked away and cared for in this clinical environment. He should be at home with them all, comforting each other, trying to make sense of this inexplicable turn of events. All of their focus had been on him and he felt responsible and isolated and so very, very sad.

***

There she was! Thomas lumbered towards the bus stop. At last he could let Mari know what was happening to Timothy. He had wanted to talk to her many times over the last few weeks but always he missed her at the bus stop and he had no means of contacting her, did not know where she lived; did not even know her last name. Of course she would have been concerned; after all she had witnessed the initial episode. Even though they weren't close friends yet, it had seemed inevitable that a romance would blossom between her and Timothy. He wasn't jealous although he would have liked a romance of his own, he was happy to see Timothy happy and Mari seemed to be a good match for his personality.

And there she was, her copper curls flowing down her back and swinging wildly as she turned to greet him. He hurried towards her,

172

recognising her from the colour of her hair rather than her features which were a blur to his myopic eyes. Unwittingly he stepped into the road, taking the most direct route to her, as he clumsily hastened his pace. He stumbled. She raised her hand and called out. A greeting? A warning? Whichever it was, he never knew. He smiled and waved to her as the vehicle slammed into his back. The force threw him to the ground and the heavy wheels ground him to a pulp. In the deathly silence that ensued, the world went black for Mari as she too felt her world turn upside down.

***

They said it was the shock that caused it. Dr Richards leant over the sleeping body and checked his heart rate, pulse and other vital signs. Satisfied that the seizure had abated and would not return, he quietly instructed Nurse Elspeth to stay with him. All her other duties were suspended for the time being. He must not be left alone. He slept, a deep sleep, a healing sleep and he dreamt…

***

"Come with me." He did not recognise the voice that whispered in his ear. The perfume was vaguely familiar but his sleepy, bandage swathed head was foggy and confused.

"Come with me." More urgent this time, he roused himself and turned toward the insistence. She bent low over his bed and held a finger to her lips, "Shhh!" In her other hand she held a robe and she lowered her raised digit and slipped her hand under his shoulders and helped him to rise up. It was easier than anticipated and there was no pain. He felt light, almost as though he were floating as she guided him down the long corridor and out through the main entrance to the hospital. No one looked up, no one watched them leave. He wanted to ask where they were going; home perhaps, as he so dearly wished. Words would not come and he understood that this was no ordinary outing. He was not afraid, he was simply curious. She smiled back at him as she held out her hand and took his, "Close your eyes," she wordlessly commanded. And as he did so, he wondered if this was just a dream but before he had time to consider further, he was swept whirling, crashing, floating, rushing through misty realms and tumbling intangibles, to arrive…

***

Thomas sat beside him. The humble room was familiar with its cosy warmth and dozens of dozing feline forms. A fire spat and crackled in the grate and he was grateful for its comfort. He could hear the wind whistling round the windows, the cry of seagulls and waves crashing against the rocks. He was not surprised to be here although he did not know how he came hither. The aroma of fresh baking assailed his nostrils and the clinking of crockery heralded the arrival of Old Bess who carried a tray of tea and scones. Behind her came Elsa and out of the shadows stepped Nurse Elspeth. The two women greeted each other briefly but with genuine delight before returning to the kitchen leaving the two boys alone with the older lady.

At first they ate and drank in silence; a comfortable silence although dripping with unasked questions. Hunger assuaged, the questions fell but Old Bess quieted them with a raised hand, "Wait!" She stood up and went to the big old oak door. As she opened it, Enigma came slinking through and pushed his wet nose into Timothy's hand; his young feathery tail wagged furiously in his obvious delight at seeing this being whom he had apparently taken it upon himself to protect. Behind him came Snowball closely followed by Peanut who waved his tail imperiously. He gave a cursory glance at Timothy and the other cats before leaping onto Thomas's lap where he rubbed himself against Thomas's cheek and curled up to sleep in his habitual way. Snowball licked Timothy's fingers in greeting and then lay at his feet. It all felt so ordinary although truth to tell, there was nothing at all ordinary about it.

"Well," began the sage, "now that we are all gathered here I should imagine you'd like some explanations." She smiled at the puzzled expressions on the boys' faces. After a brief pause, she said, "Where are…"

"Why are we…" Timothy and Thomas both began to speak at once and both hesitated as he realised.

174

"Let me fill you in a bit first and then you can ask in case I've left out parts you'd like me to expand on." Old Bess's wisdom prevailed and the two fell silent once more allowing her to continue. "You understand that your lives have been intertwined in many ways?" They nodded in agreement, "That connection is not lost because you are separated. Thomas's task in the physical world is done and that is why he has come home..."

"But he's here!" exclaimed Timothy, "Home? Surely this is not..." Thomas took his arm and leaned in to speak, "Timothy, old boy, you do know what happened don't you? Just listen to Aunty B; she is trying to help you." Timothy scowled but relaxed a little. This was all so surreal that perhaps it would be better to just go with the flow and accept. The time for questions would come later.

"Thomas will always be with you. His spirit will guide you through the rest of your time on earth. You may not see him or hear him but you will know that he is there with you, in you, round you. He is a part of you and always has been. You are not related by blood but by spirit. You each had your individual threads to weave in the great tapestry of life and for a while your paths ran side by side. Now you travel together but in one body. Timothy, yours is the hard path, but it will be the most rewarding. Fear not, for we will always be beside you, helping you to carry whatever burden is yours. You will have many experiences, some that you cannot even imagine, and others that are longed for. Nevertheless, there will be times when you will not know how to carry on, how to resolve a seemingly insurmountable problem. Call on us; we are here for you."

As she spoke, the animals rose from their rest and moved nearer to Old Bess. The cats draped themselves round her neck, on her head and across her shoulders. They climbed the bookcase behind where she sat and lay on the arms and back of the chair. They settled on her knees and at her feet. The two dogs positioned themselves at either side of her chair and they leant against her sturdy legs. Only Peanut remained where he lay. She stopped speaking and was silent. As she continued to smile at the boys in encouragement, Elsa and Elspeth appeared at her side; they did not enter the room in a conventional manner but simply appeared and were there. It was abundantly clear that her 'we' referred to them all.

Tears streamed down Thomas's still round cheeks and he muttered, "Sorry old chap" over and over until Timothy pressed his fingers to Thomas's lips. "Hey," he said softly, "it's alright. You had no choice. I understand that. It was time for you to come here – wherever here is, and this time I can't stay with you. But I think I understand what Bess is saying. I've had some strange experiences and this sort of makes sense of some of them." As he glanced up at Old Bess, he realised that three more figures had appeared behind her. Bethany, Isabelle and Eliza smiled in recognition of him and of his words. He could not have explained how he knew them, but know them he did and was comforted by their presence.

Gradually the scene before him faded; the figures blurred and became one. Elsa stepped forward and knelt before the still weeping Thomas. "Come," she said and held out her hand. They rose together and he took her proffered limb. Leaping gracefully to the floor, Peanut walked sedately to where Snowball leaned, on what was now unclear. He licked the cat's nose in greeting and followed the waving pennant of a tail to Timothy's feet. Timothy leaned down and scooped up the two fluffy figures. He buried his face alternately in their soft coats before passing the small bundles to Thomas. "Take care of him," he said, "as he has taken care of me."

"I will." The words were not spoken but the message was clear. The heavy old door creaked open and a figure in black swirled into the room. Hooded and mysterious, only the piercing blue eyes bore witness to the form beneath. He nodded briefly to where Old Bess now stood alone, and held out his arms. Elsa gave Thomas a gentle push towards the figure and then they, Thomas, Peanut and Snowball, together with the stranger, were gone.

***

"You have a visitor!" Nurse Elspeth smiled at Timothy who scowled at her in return.

"I don't want to see anyone. I told you!" he groused, "I look stupid with my half shaved head and in this ridiculous gown."

"No one cares how you look," Elspeth replied, "and in any case, I think you look quite charming. It's time you started taking an interest in something other than yourself. So come on, I'll tidy you up and let's see if we can get this robe on you. You can take her to the day room if you like."

Her? Now who could this be? The only people to visit him so far were Eleanor and Elsa and since they had only left a little while before, it was hardly likely to be either of them. Rosa, as usual, was more immersed in her own distress and her business affairs. It wasn't that she didn't care about her son; it was just that she felt he was safe where he was. The operation had been deemed a success and he was well on the way to recovery. Therefore, in her logical and practical mind, there were more pressing things to be dealt with and deal with them she must. The rest of the family was kept busy sorting out Thomas's funeral, a memorial and all the other associated businesses and necessities. In many ways he was glad to be out of it all but there were still the rankling feelings of guilt that would not abate.

***

Mari poked her head around the edge of the door. She smiled when she saw him and he thought that she looked like an angel with a copper halo. Tongue tied and unusually shy, words failed him and so it was she who led the way to the balcony outside the day room and once there, it was she who explained how she had found out where he was and what was happening.

Soon however, as Timothy relaxed and a shadow of his former confident self returned, they were chatting together as though they had known each other for a long time. Their heads bent close and their fingers occasionally brushing, it was inevitable that the meeting would end with an embrace, a kiss and a promise to meet again soon.

Chapter Thirty-Seven

Simon sat on the old bench at the edge of the park. Not for the first time he desperately wished that Tam was still here. She could always make things seem less awful. She had had a calmness about her that spilled onto others and stilled his racing thoughts. She had sailed gracefully as a swan glides over water and despite the frantic paddling of her feet below the surface, she had made everything well and poured her soothing oil on the rough waters of life. He closed his eyes and spoke to her in his heart. He asked her to once again come to him, to give him peace in this troubled time. Sometimes he felt her presence. Sometimes, inexplicably, answers came into his mind but this time there was nothing. He could not feel her...

Carrie came haltingly over the grass and plonked herself ungraciously down on the bench beside him. She took his hand and raised it to her lips, "My wuv oo Simon." She put her short, chubby arm across his shoulder and pulled his head down to rest on hers. "You mustn't feel sad," the voice was not hers, "Thomas is with me. I will take care of him here and you must look after Timothy. He is so very special and I have loved him as my own. You are the most wonderful father and the only person I could trust to look after my children. They are all my children; our children. Continue to guide them, love them and provide for them, for they need you. You are their rock and their stability in all these seemingly inexplicable times. It will not always be so traumatic. Believe me. Sometimes it will seem impossible to cope but always you will be guided. I am with you. Trust me." A pause ensued and then, "My wuv oo Simon." Carrie placed a sloppy kiss on Simon's cheek which mingled with the single tear that trickled down as he realised that he had received what he had asked for; reassurance and comfort, not just from Tam but also from Carrie who had always been so much wiser than most people understood.

***

Home at last! His initial exuberance was tempered by the absence of Thomas. He even missed the irritation of Peanut whose long hair had coated every unoccupied surface in the house. He missed Snowball too but Enigma had not left his side for more than a few moments since he had been delivered from his hospital incarceration. The young dog had quickly become part of the family and Eleanor remarked that he was remarkably like two other dogs that she had known. A vague memory of seeing Enigma in some other place hovered at the back of Timothy's mind but he did not dwell on it. It was a happy memory and he did not need to explore its depths.

***

Now where was that box? She was quite certain that it was up here in the attic somewhere. Oh bother her old bones that made bending and twisting around the numerous boxes and pieces of old furniture uncomfortable. It was cold too and she wished she were downstairs and seated in her cosy lounge. One more pile. She would investigate one more pile before she gave up for today. Two minutes later the feeble light that emanated from the small window was cut off. She stumbled in the sudden darkness but her arm was caught by a strong hand and she turned to find herself looking into the rather pale face of her grandson.

"Timothy? What are you doing up here? You should be resting not clambering around in a dusty old attic!"

"And I might say the same about you," came the retort. They laughed together and immediately felt guilty. How could they laugh when Thomas was so recently gone? In silence they made their way back down the wooden ladder into the relative warmth and light of the landing. Brushing the cobwebs from her hair and smoothing her skirts, Eleanor was elegant as always and recovered her composure as only a veteran lady can. "Come down to my rooms and we'll share a cup of tea." Her invitation was not to be refused and soon the two, young and old alike, were sipping tea and munching on freshly baked biscuits, thanks to Carrie's love of cooking and feeding her family.

"What were you looking for?" asked Timothy through a mouthful of crumbs.

"Oh, just an old photograph album. I'm sure I remember it being stored up there after Tam..." Even after all these years she could not say her daughter's name without a lump forming in her throat. Timothy looked at her sharply and he leant forward to take her hand, "Don't be upset Grandma, I think I might know what happened to it." She looked up at him and thought for the umpteenth time what a handsome boy he was and what a glorious head of hair framed those incredibly blue eyes. She smiled and waited for him to expand. He paused, his own throat momentarily closed by a matching lump, "Thomas had it," he said.

"He was scanning all the pictures onto the computer. It was part of his college course to be able to move documents and pictures around via the internet. He found the photo album and thought it would a good idea to have the pictures in a safe storage thingy on the computer. He was really good at that sort of thing." His voice tailed off and he battled to keep at bay the tears that threatened to fall. Once he had recovered himself, he promised to find the album and bring it to Eleanor before the end of the day. "I have to go out for a little while now," he apologised, "but I'll bring it to you when I get back. Is that alright?" Eleanor nodded, it was very alright. How lucky she was to have such a wonderful family around her. She stood up to embrace him and when she sat back down she closed her eyes and allowed herself the briefest moment of sorrow. Things have a way of working out as they must, this she knew, but sometimes the 'must' was oh so very painful. As if reading her thoughts, Enigma nuzzled her elbow and she absentmindedly fondled his silky ears. He had taken to watching her when his master was busy elsewhere and Eleanor appreciated his comforting and reassuring presence.

***

The wind whipped her hair where it escaped from the scarf she had wound around her head in an attempt to keep warm. The milking

180

finished and the cows safely in the byre for the cold night ahead, she made her way across the yard to the big barn. The bright red modern John Deere tractor stood where the horses had once resided. One side of the enormous engine cover was open and Tom's arms and head were buried deep inside its innards. "It's just amazing..." his words were muffled, "It's all a bit double Dutch to me but I think I can get to grips with its inner workings." Realising she would not get any attention from him while he was engrossed in his new acquisition, Sally muttered, "I'll put the kettle on then," as she left him happily tinkering and went back into the homely kitchen.

She knew where it was. She hadn't looked at it for a long time and she wasn't sure why it had come into her head today but she felt, for some unknown reason, that she needed to look at it again. Why do we get these strange compulsions? They are often inconvenient to say the least. However, up the stairs she went and into the little box room which was so rarely used. She kept it neat and tidy, if a little dusty, and there on the table beside the bed was the album exactly where she had left it several years ago following Sandra's visit. It had shocked her then and she hadn't felt any desire to look again. But now...?

***

Old Bess gazed into the deep waters of the well. Her large figure obscured the light from above and at first all that she could see was her own much wrinkled reflection. Slowly the waters stilled and she saw through them. She saw Eleanor poring over the pages of a tatty leather-bound album. Curiosity, sorrow, wonder and humour flitted across her face with each page that she turned. Sometimes she smoothed the transparent film that covered and protected each image and sometimes it seemed she stroked the figures or faces depicted but she passed swiftly on until she came to a group photograph of a man and woman and a small boy. The legend under the picture read, 'Judy, Edward and Tommy.' Old Bess could not hear the words but she knew that Eleanor was once again marvelling at the likeness between Judy and her Tam. Weren't they one and the same? Don't we all have alter egos? Nevertheless, not many of us actually come

181

face to face with ourselves. It is so difficult to explain and most people simply cannot understand how it all works.

As she looked into the well she saw Eleanor turn another page and pause again. This time a bride and groom looked out from the page. 'Ted and Miriam on their wedding day' was the legend beneath and, 'All of us' was printed below the group photograph on the opposite page. "All of those spirits, gone from that time, gone from this world," Old Bess sighed to herself. Eleanor drew the album closer to her aging eyes and Bess watched as she started in surprise. The picture became clearer to Old Bess and she smiled to herself. She knew that Eleanor had recognised the small blond boy on the far right of the picture, tucked in beside a very large black dog.

Old Bess stirred the water with a long raspberry cane. For a moment or two the images were blurred but as the waters stilled once more, she gazed upon another woman, in another place, at another time, who was also leafing through a photograph album. This album was black and equally dusty and the pictures were loose on the pages. One picture slipped unnoticed to the floor as Sally studied the images. She paused at one she had puzzled over before, Daniel and Dora gazed out at her. She was still mystified as to how they were related to Sandra's father. Perhaps it was one of those inexplicable coincidences she mused. Old Bess smiled to herself. Coincidences? Hmm...

Another page was turned, and another, and then there they were. Ted and Miriam, in their wedding finery and on the opposite page the same group photograph that Eleanor had gazed upon in that other place at that other time. Sally made a mental note to ask Sandra about her ancestors. Just as she was about to close the book, she glanced again at the group. In surprise she peered into the picture. There in the bottom right hand corner was a small blond boy leaning against a large black dog.

***

Old Bess drew back from the well and pushed her fists into her aching back. Maybe they were making connections. Maybe they were not. Maybe it didn't really matter either way but there was satisfaction in knowing that things were working as they must. In many ways it had been hard for the boys but they'd had their good times too and the bond between them would be a lasting one. They would reap their rewards in due course. Timothy would no longer suffer from the malady that had dogged his youth and Thomas was free from his ungainly and short-sighted body. Of course there were still tasks for them to complete but their purpose and destiny so far had been fulfilled.

***

It was much later, when Sally was tidying the room in readiness for a visit from Sandra and baby Mari, that she found the fallen photograph. She saw its white edge peeping out from under the bedspread where it swept to the floor. She knew the tall person at once. Austere, upright and immaculate, there, with a half-smile on her ageless face, was Bethany. "A guardian angel?" she mused, for there surely was no other explanation.

Chapter Thirty-Eight

"That's my mum?" Tom was incredulous. "Where did you find these pictures?"

Sandra laughed delightedly, "I was going through some old stuff of Mum's and there it was. I knew she had some photos because I remember seeing them when I was little but you forget who the people are. I was really only interested in seeing pictures of myself! I was looking because I wanted to know if Mari looks like any of our ancestors. Anyway, when I found that one and it looked so much like you, I did a bit of research into our family history. It's amazing what you can find out on the internet you know!" She grinned at her cousin, knowing full well that anything technological was way beyond him. He was much happier fixing engines and other mechanical devices. "Anyway, it seems that your father was the son of a couple called Ted and Miriam. The thing is they didn't really talk to each other after your grandmother died. There were rumours of drunk driving and a terrible accident after which the old boy became a recluse. He did come out of it before he died but by then he'd lost touch with your dad and that was that!" She paused to see what affect her words were having on her reserved cousin but he shrugged and indicated that she should continue since there was obviously more that she wanted to say. "Anyway, I came to ask you if you would like to be Mari's Godfather. We'd be really pleased and it seems even more appropriate now that we've realised she is to be named after your grandmother."

"What was my dad's name?" he asked.

"I'm not sure; there is a gap in the records from when Sommerset House was bombed during World War Two. It was possibly something beginning with G or maybe even T for Thomas, but I couldn't find any convincing details. Sorry." Tom was not disappointed. His parents had not been part of his life for so long that he couldn't remember them or imagine them being here and now. The names meant nothing to him although the name George might have evoked vague memories from a half forgotten dim and distant past.

"Of course, I'd be honoured to be her Godfather," he grinned at Sandra, "Let me hold her for a bit then, while she's sleeping. You can have her back when she cries!" He held out his arms and cradled the softly snuffling infant and he marvelled at her glorious head of soft, downy, copper coloured hair.

***

Eleanor sat in the front pew of the parish church. It was not her custom to attend services; she preferred to find solace in the great outdoors. Walking in the woods which had been her chapel, she found her God and communed with nature rather than with music, pomp and circumstance. However, this felt right and she was sure that Thomas would have appreciated the send-off that was given him. A simple but moving service, the memorial was a small family affair attended by the few people who had come to know and love Thomas. He was one of those people who shed love and happiness amongst the people who really knew him. Fred Barker, the now retired headmaster of Sir Randolph's, and Mr Stamp, frail and bent with age, were there as were some of the college lecturers.

Also came Heather, Lucy and Cathy, although Eleanor was not at all sure that Cathy knew who Thomas had been. They didn't stay long since Cathy was only allowed away from the home for a limited time. Many of Thomas and Timothy's shared friends from the Rugby club and Scouts paid their respects and hovering in the background, was that lovely girl who had unfortunately witnessed both incidents that had befallen the boys. As the last notes of Vidor's magnificent Toccata and Fugue died away, she breathed deeply, wiped away the last of the tears that threatened to disrupt her composure and rose from her seat. She made her way slowly across the small graveyard towards the village hall where a simple meal was awaiting the guests. These days she walked slowly and with a stick, her aging arthritic bones and dimming eyesight meant that she relied on the extra support.

Enigma appeared out of the shadows and carefully walked by her side. She no longer wondered at how he had managed to find his way out of the garden or through the village. He just did; and he was always there when he was needed no matter where there was. She was happy to accept his presence, just as Tam had accepted first Bozo and then Zulu all those years ago. More and more she found herself reminiscing about Tam and less and less did she find it upsetting to remember.

Just before she reached the lych-gate, she felt rather than saw a slight movement from behind the big Yew tree. She glanced across the mismatched and crooked headstones to where she saw shadowy figures grouped around the freshly filled grave wherein Thomas's casket had been lowered three days earlier. Slightly obscured, both by her limited sight and by the evening mist, the figures appeared to be holding hands in a circle. She watched and it seemed that as they raised their hands an indistinct shape rose with them and as they tipped their unclear faces towards the sky, the shape hovered above their heads and gradually dissipated into nothingness.

Enigma gave a slight nudge to her thigh and then a single bark at which the figures turned towards her watching form. The startled figures bowed to her and began to melt into the shadows; all except for one. Detaching itself from the group this one seemed to glide towards her and then Elsa was by her side, taking her elbow and guiding her through the gate and into the warm and bright hall where the guests awaited her.

***

Timothy, not yet fully recuperated, had been permitted to attend the burial but not the memorial. He sat disconsolately in the day room, thankful that the other patients were absent and that he had the place to himself for a while. It was very hard to be so alone. Knowing that others were celebrating the foreshortened life of his best friend, he wished that he could have at least witnessed some of the good things that were being said about his brother. He missed him most dreadfully and wondered how he could possibly go on without the constant support and subconscious knowing that Thomas had had. They hadn't needed to talk much; there had been a deep understanding between the two of them which had not needed words or discussion. Each knew when the other wanted to be alone or when a problem required two heads rather than one. At times it had almost felt as though they were one person in two bodies.

"Don't be sad. I haven't gone far." Timothy's eyes flew open at the voice. "You probably can't see me yet but I'm never far from you. Hey, no tears now! You're going to be fine. You have to carry on and finish whatever tasks are in store for you. Don't you remember Old Bess? Think about it Pal. We've always been in this together and we always will be. Cheer up and you'll soon be out of here!" Timothy blinked back the tears that temporarily blinded him and he looked around the still unoccupied room. It was only as he stood up and began to make his way back to the ward and his bed that he noticed it. He smiled. He chuckled and his amusement grew into a rich rolling laugh. And he understood. There resting on the bookshelf beside the television, standing proud in an elegant, previously non-existent, crystal vase, stood a single stem rose. Pearly white iridescence, perfectly formed, exquisitely perfumed and nestled at its heart, a solitary diamond dewdrop.

Chapter Thirty-Nine

The view was magnificent; rolling hills swept down to the valley where a silvery stream snaked sinuously through the villages until it disappeared into the vegetation which screened the dunes and the beach. Late blossom drifted down from the cherry trees and carpeted the rough lawn with pink and white petals. The half hidden and isolated chalet nestled into the side of the hill, high above the town and under the edge of the tree-line that marked the beginnings of the forest atop the crown. Camouflaged by an all-encompassing clematis creeper, the cabin was more spacious than was first apparent, although surprisingly cosy with plenty of room for all the family. A central wood-burning stove kept the chill from the cooler English evenings. It was idyllic and quiet; no traffic, no aeroplanes painting the sky with their vapour trails, no chatter from hidden workers or pleasure seekers in neighbouring gardens. And despite the cool breeze which demanded the wearing of sweaters and jackets, the sun shone.

It had been Shane's idea. They all needed a complete change, he'd said, with time to stop and absorb and adjust to all that had so recently happened. Simon, Eleanor, Elsa, Carrie and Timothy were enthusiastic but Rosa had been dubious; she really shouldn't be away from the office again. She had already taken time off to deal with the aftermath of Timothy's surgery and that time had been extended, beyond the two weeks she had allowed herself, by the tragedy that had befallen Thomas. Nevertheless, she comforted herself with the thought that if she, the boss, was unable to give herself permission to be absent for a further week, then who could? She hadn't expected the resulting situation in which she found herself...

May half-term was the best time for Shane. He was happy and successful in his chosen career. Following his years attending University, studying for a Bachelor of Arts degree in Education and, since he was Shane and never did things by halves, his Masters' degree in War History, he was fortunate to have gained a teaching

188

post at Primrose Primary School in the next town. Although his busy lifestyle rendered him conspicuous by his absence, he had been able to live at home, at Willow Lodge, until such time as he could afford a small flat for himself and his small dog. Smartie; so named for his intelligence and the round brown patches on his otherwise white back and head, went everywhere with his master and this holiday was no exception. Girls came and went but Smartie remained the only true and loyal constant in Shane's life... so far!

***

Rosa sat back in the cushioned cane rocking chair. Positioned on the semi-enclosed veranda, out of the cool breeze but in the warm, window filtered late spring sunshine; she rocked gently with one foot pressing against the corner of the matching cane coffee table. She could not stop the tears that streamed down her cheeks. She had not cried at the time. She had not cried since; not at the funeral, not at the memorial, not when helping Elsa and Eleanor to sort through his belongings, not even when they found poor Peanut, curled up on his favourite blanket box, dead. Tears were for the weak and she was not weak; she would not be weak... She brushed the deluge away and leant her head back against the chintzy cushions. But the tears would not stop and the thoughts would not diminish. She berated and admonished herself over and over again. Why had she not noticed? Why had she not given them more time? Why had she been so intent and focused on her work? Surely she must be the worst mother ever. So distressed was she that she did not notice, hear or feel his quiet approach, "Mum?" his soft voice startled her and her eyes flew open. "Timothy!" she exclaimed and hastily reached for yet another tissue.

"Mum, what has upset you so?" His gentle tone immediately encouraged another outpouring of tears and it was several minutes before she could respond. In the meantime he waited; he took her hand and gently stroked her wrist, noticing the blue, raised veins that had not been so apparent when he was a child. Age was a cruel master; one which no one can escape. Rosa, however, was as beautiful and graceful as ever. Tall and slender, with high, defined cheekbones and a strong nose and forehead, she was grace epitomised. Her dark, Hispanic looks told of her Italian roots and if you listened carefully, there was still a slight hint of an accent. After a little time, she drew a deep breath and pressed down her son's golden head to rest on her shoulder. She did not need to give an explanation to this perceptive son of hers. He knew that she was blaming herself for all that had happened. Perhaps, had she stayed at home with her baby boy, the petit mal might not have developed. Perhaps, had she stayed at home, there would not have been so many odd incidents in Timothy's young life. Perhaps, had she stayed at home she might have noticed Thomas's failing eyesight. Perhaps, had she stayed at home the responsibilities that became Eleanor's would not have aged her mother-in-law so quickly? Perhaps... perhaps.

Timothy raised his head and took both her hands in his own. He positioned himself in front of her and looked deeply into the dark pools of her brown eyes. "Close your eyes and come with me," he commanded. For a brief moment, she was puzzled and then she shrugged and closed her eyes and did as she was bid.

Swirling, rushing, floating through misty realms, she allowed herself to be guided by her son. Too distressed to resist, and too surprised to defer, she did not question him with hows and whys and wherefores, she simply followed his lead and trusted him.

"No one is perfect; no one can know what will be the effect of the choices we make. We do what seems to be the best at any given time. We do not know our purpose in this life, nevertheless, for every choice we make, for every stone we throw; ripples flow out and affect the consequential choices and actions of those that swim in the same stream. What is done is done and cannot be undone. Berating ourselves, for what we perceive to be past misjudgements or mistakes, is pointless and destructive. Instead, we should build on what is. Learn from the decisions we made and consider what might have been. But do not regret." As the shadowy figure uttered these words, tears fell ever more freely. She did not know who spoke; not her son, not anyone she recognised, however, in her heart she knew the wisdom of the lesson and of the speaker. A rough hand gently brushed away the tears and a soft kiss was placed upon her brow. A wisp of wild gray hair escaped from the hood of her cloak and the faint aroma of a combination of freshly baked bread, the great outdoors and cats, assailed Rosa's senses. "Accept what is my dear. What you have done is as right as all that has occurred. The stage was already set and the players appointed. You played your part magnificently as did the whole cast. Relax now and revel in the silent applause of angels. You may hear it in the laughter of children, the rustling of leaves on the trees, in the songs of the birds and in the sigh of the sea on sand and shingle."

"Open your eyes." The kindly spoken imperative was obeyed and Rosa observed that she was surrounded by shadowy figures that tended to her feet, her hair, her skin and her heart. She felt as though she wanted for nothing. An overwhelming alrightness filled her heart and she smiled. The familiar eyes, drilled deeply into her own, smiled back into hers and their bluest of blue gaze was intense and full of love and admiration.

***

"That's the first genuine smile I've seen on your face for a long time!" cheered Timothy, just as Shane and Carrie, closely followed by Enigma and Smartie, came tumbling up the steps to join them on the verandah. He gave his mother a quick hug and kissed her cheek before greeting his brother and sister.

"I wondered where you'd gone old boy!" Shane's concern was obvious, "Are you ok? I mean no headaches or funny turns?" he enquired.

"I'm fine," came the reply, "I just wanted to spend a bit of time with Mum, on my own, without you two stealing all the attention!" Timothy's irrepressible good humour had returned and, matched by Shane's dry wit and Carrie's gullibility, the evening passed in light-hearted banter, good food, fine wine and happy hearts.

191

Much later that night, Shane tiptoed into the kitchen. He deliberately felt his way in the dark for fear of waking Carrie who slept on the sofa-bed at the far end of the dining area. Open plan rooms were all very nice but they didn't auger well for secret midnight feasts. It was thirst that drove him to the big refrigerator and he felt his way to the dark corner where it stood. Fumbling to open the door he jumped with surprise as the overhead light was suddenly turned on and, with a resounding smash; he dropped the milk bottle that he had just taken from the now opened fridge at exactly the same moment as Carrie opened her mouth and screamed.

All hell was let loose! The dogs barked, Carrie cried, Shane laughed, Timothy shouted and Simon came charging into the small room, carrying a baseball bat and a pillow. Later there was much mirth about the pillow and exactly what function it was intended to serve! Calming Carrie was the first objective and the second and third were to clear up the spilt milk and settle the dogs. It wasn't too long before order was restored and the reluctant participants retired to resume their repose. As he passed him, on his way to the small room he shared with his wife, Simon, who didn't often openly express his feelings, grasped Shane's shoulder and squeezed it hard, saying gruffly, "It was a good idea of yours, this holiday thing. Thank you. I'm proud of you son and... and I love you."

Chapter Forty

Timothy could hardly contain his excitement. At last the long awaited day was here. The envelope would be waiting on the hall stand and then he could begin! How did he know it would be there today? That he couldn't explain – but he just knew that it would be, it had to be!

Simon slipped the keys into his pocket and patted it, just to make sure. He still had slight misgivings about all of this but the doctors had declared him fit and now there was no stopping him! It was only an old model and relatively cheap, there was bound to be some bumps and scrapes at the beginning and he could work out how to fix them for himself. It would all be a good learning curve for the boy. Boy? Why he was almost a man! The thought reminded him to wonder, as he smiled wryly to himself, who was that copper haired girl he had seen him talking to in town?

Eleanor fingered the envelope and chewed her lip. She couldn't help but worry about the lad. He'd been through so much in his short life. Was he really ready to try this? She desperately hoped it wouldn't end in yet another upside down disaster.

Elsa took the envelope from Eleanor's hands and without uttering a word placed it carefully on the hall stand.

"Is it here?" Carrie shuffled through the door, carefully carrying a plate of cookies. "My make cookies for celebrate." She smiled her gummy smile and put the plate down on the sideboard, "No' for 'oo!" she scolded Enigma.

Enigma padded to the hall and plumped down on the rug below the hall stand. He knew it was time for his master to return from college and so wait for him here he would.

Rosa hurried down the stairs. Her office was now removed from the city and established in the now spare room upstairs. The installation process had served the double purpose of entirely changing the room that had become Thomas's and it provided her with a more than satisfactory work space. Since their return from the holiday, she had revised her hours and her workload. She had delegated many of her tasks to her excellent assistant and as a result she was happier, more rested and much more involved in everyday family life. She had even considered suggesting that there was no longer any need for Elsa's position. The suggestion, however, had died as soon as it formed; there was absolutely no way that Elsa could leave them – was there? She was as much a part of the family as everyone else.

The only time or way that she could go elsewhere was if and when she chose to do so. She smiled at the girl, noticing as she did so that she was a girl no longer. A hint of grey streaked the woman's hair and fine lines around her eyes betrayed the truth of her maturity. Catching her elbow as she passed by, Rosa swung Elsa round to face her. "You do know how very grateful I am to you for all that you do for all of us?" In response Elsa smiled and briefly hugged her superior, "I wouldn't have it any other way," she whispered, "this is where I'm mean't to be."

He bounced through the door, dropped his bag, kicked off his shoes, threw his jacket, which missed, at the hall chair, absently patted Enigma on the top of his head and grabbed the envelope. "It's here!" he shouted triumphantly. He ripped open the brown envelope and casting it aside, drew out the small pale green plastic card which bore, in miniature, some numbers, his photograph, his signature and in the top left had corner, a red L. Crashing into the lounge, leaving his trail of destruction behind him, he was greeted by the entire family who were cheering, smiling and clapping. Carrie proffered the plate of cookies and Timothy took one and stuffed it whole into his mouth before he gave her a crumby kiss on the cheek. He hugged Eleanor and Rosa and then turned to Elsa and Shane before noticing that Simon had left the room. He was about to enquire as to where he had gone when he heard the sound of a throaty engine and the crunch of gravel as a vehicle turned into the driveway.

It was perfect. It was exactly what he had hoped for. Bright red, glossy, sleek lines, gleaming chrome trims and white leather seats and best of all, the little Mazda sports car had an open top! Of course the illusion was slightly marred by the necessity of Learner plates on the bumpers fore and aft, but it was his and he was ecstatic.

Six months later, after suffering the indignity of having to have Elsa, Rosa, Shane or Simon riding beside him, he was finally free to exchange his green plastic card for a pink one, with no L on it, and to take his pride and joy for a spin on his own.

The wind whistled through his, still blond and curly, hair. Not for him the fashionable shaved look that his compatriots were adopting. No, he preferred to leave his hair naturally wild and a little too long. Not that he ever really thought about his looks and he certainly didn't consider fashion. If he was comfortable he was happy. Nevertheless, he had a naturally suave appearance and at twenty years old, his childish chubbiness was replaced with a lean angularity and well defined muscle tone that had all the girls swooning. Despite this he was more or less ignorant of the effect that he had on the so called fairer sex and was totally indifferent to their reactions to him. There was one however who intrigued him.

Since her visit to the hospital, he had seen very little of Mari. It was not his intention to ignore or avoid her but somehow life and busyness got in the way of social interactions. He had seen her once or twice at the bus stop after he had resumed his college studies but the term ended, the exams were taken and the desired results achieved. Also, since his acquisition of the little red car, there had been fewer occasions on which he needed to travel by bus. His family had been very supportive and were willing to inconvenience themselves in order to accompany him, whilst he was still a learner driver, on his various trips to college, and so there had rarely been any need to revert to communal public transport. He had met her once or twice, by accident, in town and once they had shared a lunch break in the little cafe by the station.

**

There was no mistaking that glorious head of copper curls. He slowed the car and carefully brought it to a stop just beyond the edge of town. She stepped up to the driver's door and bent to rest her forearms on the top of the raised window. Her hair fell forward through the open top and the wind whisked it into his face as she greeted him with a wide smile. Grinning, he patted the seat beside him and offered to take her for a spin. She nodded her head, making the coiled ringlets bounce, and skipped around the car before slipping into the passenger's seat, "I haven't got much time to spare but you can give me a lift home if you like." It seemed a brilliant idea to Timothy. At last he would find out where she lived and maybe he could raise the courage to ask her out on a date. He wasn't quite sure why he found it so difficult but find it so he did. He would work out how to ask her, what to say, while he was driving her home...

**

The wind whistled through her hair and whipped it across her face before she raised her hand and held it down while she tied a scarf around her head. The road between this town and hers was long and straight and gave ample opportunity for safely showing off the capabilities of his most prized possession. He wouldn't drive too fast; he didn't want to frighten her and he didn't want to risk an accident. He pressed his foot gently on the accelerator and the well-tuned engine responded with a satisfying growl. Gradually the speedometer crept round the dial; sixty, seventy, eighty miles per hour; time to slow down for the little hump-backed bridge. He eased his foot from the throttle but the car did not slow down. Instead the speed seemed to increase and he watched in astonishment as the speedometer continued to move inexorably nearer to full circle. Ninety, one hundred, one hundred and ten; now he was frightened; he couldn't breathe, he couldn't speak, he pressed his foot on the brake pedal but nothing, no response. One hundred and twenty, one hundred and thirty; he glanced at her, but she was smiling and laughing, without any evident fear in her expression. He closed his eyes and prayed, "Dear God! Save us, please?" He felt the wheels lift from the ground; or rather he became aware of an absence of rumble from the tyres on tarmac. Were they flying? How could this be?

"Relax," the voice he knew, "remember what you know. Yours is not a conventional path. You are protected. You will not come to harm and whilst she is with you, neither will she. You must take care of her. She is yours. You are hers. Your togetherness is the culmination of all that you have experienced. Understand this."

He dared to open one eye just a fraction. They were indeed flying, high above the clouds. There far below them, little white puffs were scattered above the green fields of the English countryside. Mari still laughed delightedly and pointed down to a little old stone cottage which clung to the rocks high above the sea. She mouthed something to him but he could not hear her words. His head began to swim and in fear he thought that his malady had returned. As he shook his head to clear the threatening fogginess, he looked down to where she pointed. There, far below, stood a diminutive figure. Wisps of gray hair and her apron flapping in the wind, Old Bess waved a handkerchief in salutation.

***

Peace and comfort flowed through his veins and as the swathe of sleep began to lift, he gradually became aware of her hand stroking his hair and her green eyes smiling down into his where his head lay cushioned in her lap. The plaid picnic rug was spread on the grassy headland. Soft sand flowed over the dunes and down to the long and vacant beach. Behind the dunes a band of lightly wooded grassland sloped upward and curved to the left into the rocky foothills of seemingly inhospitable and formidable mountains. To the far right a silvery stream snaked its way across the sand and spilled its freshness into the sea. In the still air the sound of water over rocks and through grassy passes provided musical accompaniment to the songs of small birds and the cries of small creatures.

The slumber sloughed from his senses and a light breeze stirred the stillness causing Mari to pull her cotton cardigan more closely about her shoulders. "Perhaps we should go back now?" He did not want to break the magic of this moment. He drew her mouth down to his and kissed her long and deeply. He felt her body respond as did his and emptiness flowed through him when she pulled away and gently, wordlessly chided him. She didn't speak again but began to gather up the remnants of a picnic and pack it away into a wicker hamper. It did not occur to him to question how they came to be in this place or from whence came the rug or hamper. He simply accepted what was and helped her to fold the blanket. He took the basket from her and hand in hand they made their way across the grassland to where a glint of red indicated the location of their means of getting home.

He placed the hamper on the carrier above the boot and capably strapped it down as though he had done it many times before. He helped her into the passenger seat, knowing that the place was hers. Sliding confidently in behind the steering wheel he inserted the key into the ignition. Just as he was about to turn the key, she placed her hand possessively on his thigh and leant across to whisper into his ear, "The answer is yes! I do, I will, I am." Despite having no recollection whatsoever of having asked the question, he knew exactly to what she referred. He kissed her again and between each phrase as he replied, "I do love you, I will marry you and I am yours forever too."

Chapter Forty-One

"My very dear Grandson, Timothy and your beautiful Bride, Tamara,

Treasure what you have for in the blink of an eye your whole world can be turned upside down!

I do not presume to pour cold water on your happiness, I merely wish to share with you a very little of what I have understood about the world in which we live and our purpose in being here.

We each experience differently. Natural, global disasters such as earthquakes, tsunamis and volcanic eruptions, manmade disasters such as traffic accidents, wars and terrorism, affect us all to some extent, but often at a distance. And yet, much closer to home, the simple things, a birth, a death, a romance, a tragedy, an unprecedented achievement; surely none of these things leave us untouched. It is a poor man indeed who can ignore the impact of life changing events. We deal with these occurrences in our individual ways and it is the consequence of our dealings that make us who we are and that guide us in our future decision making. Life is full of lessons; we can choose to learn or we can sail sublimely through our lives taking what we will and ignoring what we won't accept. I do not presume to tell you which is the correct way; the right path, you must find your own answers.

However, it seems to me that we are guided; that we are offered choices and we are given the tools with which to make those choices. We have only to listen to our inner selves, to consider with great care what might be the consequences of the various choices on offer and to be flexible and kind in our dealings with other people and their differing opinions.

I do not have a successful and long lasting personal relationship on which to base my views but I have observed and noted much about the people who have coloured my life, both here at home and in the wider world around us. In many ways I have been privileged and have not suffered unduly in a physical sense. There have been bad times of course, losing my beloved Tamarind was almost unbearably awful, but I have been blessed with a loving family to support me and with spiritual guidance about which you know more than most. Will you read the ramblings of an old woman and think about what I have written?

Consider those people who celebrated that happy day with us just last week? Many of them were strangers both to me and to you. Elderly relations have a habit of appearing at weddings and funerals! We live our lives more-or-less oblivious of their existence and yet they are bound inextricably to us and we can learn so much from them if only we take the time and trouble to know their stories.

Did you notice the gentleman who was confined to a wheelchair? Did you notice the empty space where his right leg should have been? What is his story? Mari's grandfather, Tomo, lost his leg in wartime, that much we do know, but what is his story? How was he guided, how did he come to terms with such tragedy? No! Don't look for answers, just consider and reflect; could you have accepted such a fate?

Of course we all have our crosses to bear and none knows that better than you my dearest Timothy. I do not judge you, remember the little green soldier with the matchstick leg...?

Sandra – Mari's wonderful mother; such colour and flamboyance in her dress, but did you see the sadness behind her eyes? And Tom, her cousin, perhaps it is their 'aloneness' that is their strength? They have each other and they have their partners but in their darkest hours they had no one to lean on;

200

no one to help carry their burdens. And yet they were not beaten; they were not entirely abandoned. Just as there have been spirits supporting me, I'm sure that they were also guided and helped when they needed it most. How do I know these things? I listen, I look, I learn.

Unwrap your gift from her and you will see that Sally has woven all of these things into an exquisite cloth that will adorn your table and remind you each time you look at it, just how much we are helped by those we do not always recognise or acknowledge.

Timothy – oh how we have loved, and laughed, and wondered and worried... You remind me so much of my Tam and yet you are not of her flesh or blood. I know that things work in mysterious ways and I know that you and she are linked through some unfathomable bond. Perhaps it will be made clear to me someday, perhaps not. You have had more to contend with than many others and to lose Thomas as you have... my heart cries for you. And yet you have born it with such fortitude, I sometimes feel that you have not lost him at all, that he is with you now and always will be. I still marvel at the extraordinary circumstance that was revealed by Uncle Phillip. Who would have guessed that Thomas was more closely related to me than you ever were! Though still not of my flesh, he, like you was of my heart.

Forgive the wanderings of my poor old mind! You have better things to do with your time I'm sure. However, there is a little more I would like you to read...

Tam once tried to explain to me some of the extraordinary occurrences that she experienced. I think that you have a better understanding of what she attempted to describe than I will ever have. I have watched you as I had watched her and I see parallels that others would perhaps not notice. I want to say to you what, in the past, I have said to her -

201

You are so much more than just blood and muscle and bone. There is a light, powerful, and loving spirit that lives within you. Fill that spirit with all those experiences such as I mentioned at the beginning of this too long missive and use them to guide you into a long and satisfying future together. When you are done with this world, your spirit will carry your learning into whatever comes afterwards. Nurture and love yourself as well as you love each other. Things happen for reasons even when we cannot know what those reasons are. Accept what is and change only what you must. Don't interfere; observe and let things happen.

Finally, (I am almost done!) I found this little story on the internet when I was playing with Elsa's laptop. I was proud of myself for being able to find my way around in all that technology! Anyway, here it is to guide you.

'After a long and tiring day at work a man sat down to his dinner. On his plate was a piece of burnt toast and beside it a knife and some jam. His son watched warily and wondered what his father would say to his wife. The father said nothing but picked up the burnt toast, spread it with jam and began to eat. A little while later, the boy's mother apologised for the burnt toast and the father hugged her.

Later that night, as his father tucked him up in bed, the boy asked, "Dad, do you like burnt toast?" The father kissed the boy's forehead and replied, "Your mother has had a long and difficult day. She is tired." And as the boy made to ask another question, he pressed his finger against his son's lips and said, "Burnt toast never hurt anyone but unkind words can stab you to the heart."

Remember this, my children. There will be times when a sharp retort or criticism springs to your lips but consider before you speak because you never know what damage your apparently perfectly reasonable remark might do to someone else's feelings.

And with that little homily, I must end. Live, love, laugh and be happy but always consider these words that, in truth, are not mine but are borrowed from Harpur Lee's 'To Kill a Mocking Bird'; 'you do not know what someone else is experiencing until you have walked a mile in their shoes!'

My very sincerest congratulations, much love and very best wishes for a long and fulfilling future together,

Eleanor xxx"

Chapter Forty-Two

Her frustration could be seen in her eyes and in her hands as she plucked ineffectually at the crocheted blanket that covered her knees. No words came from the lopsided mouth and the thick tongue dribbled saliva onto a muslin cloth that was tucked into the high neck of her old-fashioned cotton nightgown. Elsa attended quietly to her needs; mopping her eyes and her chin and carefully raising her head as she held the delicate tea cup to her lips. The thoughtfully provided sipping cup had been violently thrown aside by the strongly resentful lady and her preference for her habitual china was made abundantly obvious. It is amazing how clearly it is possible to communicate without words; but only when it comes to simple things. For the most part Eleanor was trapped in her damaged brain which refused, point blank, to cooperate with her wishes; her leg and arm persistently failed to obey her commands to move as she desired and her mouth would not form the words she wished to say.

It was Rosa who had found her that morning. On her way out for an early swim in the morning sunshine, before the crowds descended on the lake, she had popped her head around Eleanor's bedroom door and was astonished to find the bed empty. It was unheard of these days for Eleanor to be up before eight o'clock in the morning, but there she was, gone! Something made Rosa hesitate. She had been on the point of leaving the room when a sound or a slight movement alerted her to the fact that something more than an empty bed was amiss. She moved from the doorway and her view opened out to include the whole bed, rather than just the side nearest the window. A foot protruded from behind the ottoman which stood at the end of the bed; a foot with a shoe on it; the same shoe that Eleanor had been wearing the night before. This puzzled Rosa since Eleanor was meticulous about her toilet and would not have slept either on the floor or with her shoes on and she certainly hadn't been inebriated. With her heart beating rather more rapidly than usual, she crossed the room in a few quick strides and gasped as she saw her mother-in-law lying prostrate, on her back, her tongue lolling, her eyes staring and totally incapable of getting back on her feet.

Elsa came running at Rosa's cry. An ambulance was called; after Elsa had examined her thoroughly for damaged limbs, Simon and Shane lifted Eleanor carefully onto the bed and Carrie was sent on some insignificant errand in order to keep her from panicking.

It was confirmed later that morning that Eleanor had suffered a stroke from which she was unlikely to fully recover. Nevertheless, the skill and attentiveness of the medical staff and the support of the family meant that in less than a fortnight, Eleanor was home to be looked after by Elsa for as long as she needed care. There was never any question of her going into a nursing home. This was her home, here at Willow Lodge, and at home she would remain until such time as the care she needed could no longer be provided.

Gradually, the family came to terms with the changes in the household. Timothy and Mari returned from their honeymoon to find things irrevocably altered and despite their dismay at Eleanor's altered circumstances, were privately pleased that arrangements had been made for them to make their home in the apartment above the garage, which had been vacated by Shane and left empty for some time. Setting aside their sorrow, they began the process of redecorating and furnishing the two roomed space and making it their own.

Carrie took it upon herself to become Eleanor's spokesperson. She had an unerring instinct for knowing precisely what Eleanor wanted and seemed to be able to accurately predict what was needed even before Eleanor herself had realised. She and Elsa made Eleanor's life as comfortable as possible and apart from the absence of Eleanor's dulcet tones speaking quietly to whomsoever was available to listen to her wisdoms, life went on.

Enigma, in accepting his master's change of allegiance from his dog to his wife, similarly transferred his loyalties to a mistress who needed companionship and comfort. He lay at Eleanor's feet night and day and was only persuaded to leave her side to eat, to exercise and to relieve himself outside from time to time. Often Eleanor's 'good' hand could be found with her fingers entwined in the thick hair at the base of his neck, or gently caressing his long and silky ears, while he gently 'grumbled' in ecstasy.

Rosa continued to join Eleanor for their customary cup of tea each afternoon. It was a habit they had established early in their, now long, association and she saw no reason as to why it should be any different. At four o'clock each day, Carrie carefully carried a tea tray into Eleanor's sitting area. The teacups were the best porcelain, the spoons silver, the milk jug, sugar bowl and tongs neatly arranged and always a plate of cookies, scones, fairy cakes or shortbread was temptingly included. Rosa would follow with the teapot; it being too hot to entrust to Carrie's clumsy administration, and would pour tea for two. Elsa remained to assist with the raising of the cup to Eleanor's lips and to mop up drips and crumbs as they fell.

On this particular day, Eleanor was agitated and it was clear that she was trying to communicate something to Rosa. Her hand waved vaguely in the direction of her bureau and her eyes followed her hand appealing to Rosa to understand. As soon as Carrie returned to clear away the remnants of the tea, she looked at Eleanor and followed her eyes, "In vere," she explained, "somefing in vere. Gamma want oo take it out." Eleanor smiled a lopsided grin and her head wobbled in agreement. Quickly Rosa went to the bureau and opened it. The first thing she saw was the letter addressed to Mr and Mrs Timothy Cooper. Next to the letter was a resin paperweight which encased a single white rose; the twin to another that had been given by Sally as a wedding present to the happy couple. Picking up the letter she held it out to Eleanor who nodded and her eyes flicked again towards the desk. Rosa took up the paperweight and her eyes looked questioningly at Eleanor. "Give me 'em." Carrie held out her hands, "My take 'em to 'em." Rosa placed the two items, one heavy, the other light as a feather, into Carrie's hands and she went.

***

Timothy sat with the crisp white, copperplate adorned paper held lightly in his fingers and his hands hung down. On the table beside him stood the two, matching, beautifully enclosed blooms. Tears fell freely and Mari stood behind his hunched shoulders methodically massaging his broad back. Hanging from a silver chain fastened around her neck and touching his cheek gently as she rhythmically swayed, was a smooth golden pebble. "My amazing grandmother..." was all he could mutter, "...Oh so wise. So very, very wise."

Chapter Forty-Three

Pearly white iridescence, perfectly formed, exquisitely perfumed
and nestled at its heart, a solitary diamond dewdrop;
the aged rambling rose put forth
a single bloom.

Shadowy figures worked tirelessly. Their preparations were almost done. All was well and nothing was forgotten.

Old Bess worked diligently pruning the rambling brambles that threatened to overwhelm the stone walls of the old cottage. Secateurs poised, she hesitated as she breathed in the exquisite perfume that emanated from that last, perfect bloom of the summer, but she knew what must be done and so the scissors snipped the thorny stem.

A little while later the door to the old cottage swung open and Old Bess hobbled through, skirts swirling in the breeze, multifarious cats scattered and Snowball, the little white dog, raised his head in greeting. She busied herself making preparations in the homely kitchen. They would be here soon and all must be ready.

The first to arrive were Bethany, Liza and Isabella. They were soon followed by Eliza, Elsa and Elspeth. A tinkling laugh announced the presence of Lizzie until Elizabeth joined her and quieted the curly haired child. More guests arrived in the shape of Peanut and Enigma, Bozo, and Zulu. You would have found it hard to distinguish between the three black dogs for they were so alike. They were greeted in turn and with varying degrees of enthusiasm by Snowball who never did quite come to terms with his long term feline companion, Peanut. Despite the confined space available in the old cottage, there was plenty of room for all. No words were spoken; embraces were given, smiles exchanged and a general air prevailed; of satisfaction in a job well done. Tea was supped, scones consumed and, as darkness fell, farewells were bid. One-by-one, each figure drew around them their cloak, bowed to the assembled company and was gone until all that were left were the old lady and her equally elderly dog.

As darkness fell the two aged and venerable beings made their way haltingly out into the small flagged yard that overlooked the wild sea. Old Bess drew back the cover from the ancient stone well and wound the creaking handle to raise the wooden bucket. Lifting it aside, she leaned over the rim and drew her cloak over her head to see more clearly into the murky waters below. The small dog lapped gently from the rickety container of still, pure water.

She smiled in satisfaction as she saw what had been done and knew that it was good; not perfect, but just as it should be. This chapter in her work was completed and she should draw a line under the final words. And as one chapter closes so another must open as the great wheel of life turns and turns.

Timothy, she mused, had reached a plateau; a pausing point. There would be more for him to do but for now he could revel in his new found contentment with Mari, with whom he was destined to share his life; his love. Indeed, hadn't this union been precisely that for which he had been unwittingly and partially responsible? Of course he had no idea of just how essential had been his purpose; his guidance; his suffering. God works in a mysterious way; isn't that what is said? Whether you believe in God or not, life is most certainly a mystery and some things will remain unexplained even beyond the end. Coincidences, strange occurrences, forgotten moments, all combine to colour the rich tapestry of our lives.

Eleanor? Eleanor was nearing the end of this journey. It was not quite her time to set out on the next, but her old soul was tiring, her physical being worn out and her emotional reserves exhausted. She had achieved so much and given so much; her love and wisdom were poured as oil on the sometimes troubled waters of her unconventional family. Perhaps it was a time now for some of them to repay her kindness and caring. They would have the opportunity for a little while and then...

Reaching into her vast apron pocket she drew out the single white rose. She smiled to herself as her lips framed the words, "Thy will be done." She held the exquisite blossom up to the moon by which light it seemed to swirl and glow pink and gold. Swiftly and purposefully she extended her arm over the rustic circular stone orifice and as she breathed the words, "On earth as it is in Heaven," she tossed the iridescent bloom into the dark depths. She watched as it tumbled and turned toward the sparkling reflection far, far below, "...forgive us our trespasses as we forgive," she murmured.

***

The small boy was engrossed in his miniature empire which for him was a whole other world. It was a universe in which he was God and it was for him to decide who lived and who died, what went where and how it would all begin and all end. And as he played another figure joined the first and the two blonde heads bowed low together over the miniature empire...

It was the perfume that first assailed his senses. He raised his head and smiled a beatific smile. He looked up to the blue sky above and watched as the delicate, iridescent, pearly white, perfectly formed, exquisitely perfumed, diamond centred flower tumbled and turned as it fell. The single bloom, put forth by the aged rambling rose, now lay, completely out of place and upside down in the wet and muddy puddle...

The Author

Janet Ollerenshaw is a retired English/Music teacher and the mother of seven children. Although recently relocated to a very small rural village near Oundle, Northamptonshire, she has lived in Hertfordshire, England for most of her life. She has been involved with music, stagecraft, scouting, outdoor activities, animals and arts and crafts alongside her long teaching career and is now enjoying having the time and freedom to write, to travel and to sing.

Janet writes for pleasure and enjoys word-craft; hence her writing can be prosaic at times since she feels that the experience of reading should be more than just a good story; rather like a good wine is one that touches senses other than simply taste and satisfaction. She has a Masters' degree in Educational Research, focused on self-esteem for learning, from Cambridge University and studied with the Open University for her first Degree in Humanities with Music and with English Language. She currently does occasional/seasonal work as an English exam marker for Pearson and for Cambridge International Exam board. She enjoys spending time in the company of her elderly parents, her numerous grandchildren and her garden.

Printed in Great Britain
by Amazon